PRAISE FOR GREGG HURWITZ

NEMESIS

"*Nemesis* is an excellent turning point in the *Orphan X* series, with great story arcs that embrace meaningful and engaging themes distinct to each character and also open the door for an even rawer and emotionally beaten Evan like you would never expect by the end of the narrative. Hurwitz throws a curveball that will leave you stunned for the better part of a day when you finally reach the end."

—Best Thriller Books

LONE WOLF

"Gregg Hurwitz seems to have found a new gear as he kicks things up a notch, ramping up the action and tension to deliver the most fascinating and compelling *Orphan X* novel to date. Think Jason Bourne on steroids . . . *Lone Wolf* is one of the year's first must-read thrillers."

—The Real Book Spy

"The series has always been a blend of Batman, the Equalizer, and Vince Flynn's Mitch Rapp, and *Lone Wolf* reinforces why it continues to be great nine novels in. Newcomers to Evan's adventures should feel fine starting here before diving into the others."

—First Clue

"*Lone Wolf* is a crushingly brilliant piece of fiction."

—Best Thriller Books

"There is simply no one writing thrillers like Gregg Hurwitz . . . Evan Smoak, the fascinating, richly imagined protagonist at the heart of the *Orphan X* series, leaps off the page. If you haven't read Gregg Hurwitz, you're missing out."

—Lisa Unger

"You can never go wrong with an *Orphan X* book. No, scratch that. An *Orphan X* book will never fail to blow your fucking mind."

—Best Thriller Books

"Hurwitz continues to dazzle."

—*Booklist*

"Another crackling caper for the solitary Orphan X."

—*Kirkus Reviews*

"Reading an *Orphan X* tale is truly a guilty pleasure, akin to eating dessert before dinner."

—*Mystery and Suspense Magazine*

"The suspense that builds surrounding the final battle . . . keeps driving *Lone Wolf* forward with the velocity of a speeding bullet . . . This might be his best *Orphan X* thriller yet."

—Bookreporter

OUT OF THE DARK

". . . honestly the best thing Hurwitz has ever written!"

—The Real Book Spy

"The plotting is clever, the action is nearly constant and usually over the top, and X has something resembling a moral core. Bad guys get what bad guys deserve . . . Hurwitz fans will certainly enjoy this latest entry in the series."

—*Kirkus Reviews*

"Evan Smoak roars back with a vengeance in the fourth *Orphan X* thriller . . . this installment is as tightly plotted, efficiently written, and, yes, as curiously plausible as its predecessors. If Jack Reacher fans haven't checked out Smoak yet, they're missing a sure bet."

—Booklist

DARK HORSE

"Nonstop action and relentless pacing are matched by deeply philosophical and powerfully emotional undertones . . . This series just gets better as it evolves."

—Publishers Weekly, starred review

"Hurwitz gives his seventh *Orphan X* thriller an epic scope, writing with verve and color . . . A crackerjack thriller that briskly enhances the legend of *Orphan X*."

—Kirkus Reviews

"One of thrillerdom's most compelling characters . . . another surefire hit."

—Booklist

"Hurwitz has a way of writing action-adventure shoot-up scenes like no other author. This one keeps you on the edge of your seat (like all his books do)."

—Red Carpet Crash

"This violent action thriller has a pleasing moral conundrum that lifts it above the usual revenge tales."

—*The Sun*

"Awesome and propulsive as the others—big Bourne and Reacher energy."

—*The New York Times*

"Evan Smoak always has some trick up his sleeve. He's far from your typical action hero, and his mix of smarts and stubbornness continues to be a winning combination."

—Bookreporter

"A riveting action adventure from first page to last, *Dark Horse* by Gregg Hurwitz is a deftly scripted novel that will have special appeal for fans of vigilante-style justice. The stuff of which blockbuster movies are made, *Dark Horse*, the seventh title in the author's *Orphan X* series, is a truly memorable read and highly recommended."

—The Midwest Book Review

"The perfectly paced and beautifully structured *Dark Horse* is like a Reacher tale on steroids. The action set pieces are masterworks of form and function, and Smoak has evolved into the quintessential lone gunman, not a lot of bark but a whole lot of bite. Thrillers don't get any better than this."

—The Providence Journal

THE LAST ORPHAN

"There is simply no one writing thrillers like Gregg Hurwitz. He's a beautiful writer who dives deep into character but never takes his foot off the gas when it comes to action and suspense. If you haven't read Gregg Hurwitz, you're missing out."

—Lisa Unger, *New York Times* bestselling author of *The New Couple in 5B*

"Just when I thought the *Orphan X* novels couldn't get any better, Gregg Hurwitz takes the series to an even higher level. *The Last Orphan* is pulse pounding, heart stopping, and thought provoking. I loved it."

—Meg Gardiner, #1 *New York Times* bestselling author

"*The Last Orphan* is a top-notch thriller and action-packed joyride. Readers will not want to put it down."

—Karin Slaughter, *New York Times* and international bestselling author

"The writing is crisp, the action scenes are both clever and cinematic, the dialogue is pitch perfect, and the villains are deliciously detestable. First class."

—*Booklist*

"This is another great *Orphan X* novel filled with the dramatic moments, fights, shoot-outs, and witty writing that we have come to love in this series. Fans of X will be very happy."

—Red Carpet Crash

"Gregg Hurwitz has never taken his foot off the gas pedal. *The Last Orphan* continues his trend of complex thrills with an engaging protagonist."

—*Bookreporter*

"*The Last Orphan* has it all . . . a story that has more unexpected twists and turns than a Disney World rollercoaster."

—Midwest Book Review

"Reading an Evan Smoak tale is truly a guilty pleasure, like eating dessert before dinner . . . Hurwitz proves to be a master storyteller as he uncouples this riveting barn burner of a thriller."

—*Mystery and Suspense Magazine*

"Another smart thriller from a master of the genre."

—*Winnipeg Free Press*

PRODIGAL SON

"Simply the best all-out action writer in the business, to which he adds a shrewd sense of character . . . Not to be missed."

—*The Providence Journal*

"An impressive addition to the outstanding *Orphan X* series."

—Shelf Awareness

"With *Prodigal Son*, Hurwitz proves once more that he's one of the most gifted authors working in the genre today. If you're not reading this series, don't wait a second longer."

—The Real Book Spy

"If you read *Prodigal Son*, you will be a fan of Hurwitz for life."

—Bookreporter

"One hell of a series . . . Nuanced and energetic, this is a great thriller."

—*Booklist* (starred review)

"*Prodigal Son* is further proof that Gregg Hurwitz has cornered the market on first-rate thrillers."

—*New York Journal of Books*

"The pacing is breathtakingly brisk throughout, and the action is relentless . . . This series continues to impress."

—*Publishers Weekly*

"Fans of Tom Clancy or Lee Child will love this latest installment . . . which offers twists and turns, danger and adrenaline, and gadgetry worthy of James Bond."

—*Library Journal*

"Read the *Orphan X* series. You'll thank me later."

—David Baldacci

"A stellar series . . . The stories get better with each installment."

—Associated Press

"Nobody walks the line between blistering action and searing character development better than Hurwitz."

—*The Providence Journal-Bulletin*

HELLBENT

"*Hellbent* is carved from the same cloth of not only Lee Child but also David Baldacci, and it proves Hurwitz to be every bit the equal of both of them. This is raw, visceral action writing layered with rare depth and emotion, making *Hellbent* an early contender for one of the best thrillers of the year."

—*The Providence Journal*

"A beautifully crafted story that builds on the previous two books in surprising and unsettling ways."

—*Winnipeg Free Press*

"*Hellbent* is Gregg Hurwitz firing on all cylinders."

—*The Guardian* (UK)

"Must-read!"

—*New York Post*

"Where there's Smoak, there's firepower. The only thing better than a great book is a series in which each book is exponentially better than the last. It's not a feat that can be pulled off by just any author, but it's viscerally powerful when done right, and *Hellbent* is as right as it gets."

—*The Oklahoman*

"This is a great novel . . . do not miss this one."

—*Booklist* (starred review)

"As well done as the rest of the series and bloody good fun."

—*Kirkus Reviews*

"This one is personal . . . Fans of the first two books will enjoy this nail-biting, twisty thriller."

—*Library Journal*

THE NOWHERE MAN

"Superb on all levels and a must-read for all thriller fans."

—*Providence Journal*

"Beautifully rendered . . . genius at work."

—*Winnipeg Free Press*

"Hurwitz knows how to put the reader deep in the mind of his hero as the pace never lets up."

—Associated Press

"Will keep readers on the edge of their seats . . . Hurwitz's engaging, sympathetic characters place this thriller above the pack."

—*Publishers Weekly* (starred review)

"A brilliant sequel. As good as *Orphan X* was, this is an even better novel, mostly because of its more claustrophobic setting, its captivating villain, and the way the author keeps ratcheting up the danger, including one really clever twist near the end of the book. Where there's Smoak, there's fire—and plenty of it."

—*Booklist* (starred review)

"Fans of Jack Reacher will love Evan Smoak, a man who will do anything to aid the innocent (something he never was)."

—*Library Journal*

ORPHAN X

"This isn't simply Hurwitz's 'best thriller yet' or 'a terrific new thriller'—*Orphan X* is an order-of-magnitude leap into stardom. It's the most exciting thriller I've read since *The Bourne Identity*. Fans of Jack Reacher, Mitch Rapp, and Jason Bourne will LOVE Evan Smoak, and the deadly, secret world of the Orphan Program. A new thriller superstar is born!"

—Robert Crais

"What is *Orphan X*? A thrill-a-minute read with twists and turns galore. I'm looking forward to Evan Smoak's next adventure."

—Phillip Margolin

"*Orphan X* is the most gripping, high-octane thriller I've read in a long, long time. Hang on to your seat because Gregg Hurwitz will take you on a dizzying ride you'll not soon forget!"

—Tess Gerritsen

"Gregg Hurwitz's *Orphan X* is his best yet—a real celebration of all the strengths he brings to a thriller."

—Lee Child

"From the explosive opening, where a boy begins his dramatic transformation, *Orphan X* blows the doors off most thrillers I've read and catapults the readers on a cat-and-mouse chase that feels like a missile launch. Brilliantly conceived and plotted, his character Evan Smoak, *Orphan X*, deserves his own niche in the thriller-hero hall of fame. Read this book. You will thank me later."

—David Baldacci

"*Orphan X* is the most exciting new series character since Jack Reacher. And Reacher would love this guy. A page-turning masterpiece of suspense enriched by compassion and insight."

—Jonathan Kellerman

"Exciting and mind blowing! A perfect mix of Jason Bourne and Jack Reacher, ex-operative Evan Smoak turns on the action and shows off all the right moves as he sets out to help the downtrodden and perhaps save his own humanity along the way."

—Lisa Gardner

THE DELIVERY

ALSO BY
GREGG HURWITZ

Orphan X Series

Orphan X

The Nowhere Man

Hellbent

Out of the Dark

Into the Fire

Prodigal Son

Dark Horse

The Last Orphan

Lone Wolf

Nemesis

Antihero

Stand-Alones

The Tower

Minutes to Burn

Do No Harm

The Crime Writer

Trust No One

You're Next

They're Watching

The Survivor

Tell No Lies

Don't Look Back

THE DELIVERY

a novella

GREGG HURWITZ

THOMAS & MERCER

Text copyright © 2026 by Gregg Hurwitz
All rights reserved.

Published by Thomas & Mercer, Seattle

www.apub.com

Amazon, the Amazon logo, and Thomas & Mercer are trademarks of Amazon.com, Inc., or its affiliates.

EU product safety contact:
Amazon Media EU S. à r.l.
38, avenue John F. Kennedy, L-1855 Luxembourg
amazonpublishing-gpsr@amazon.com

ISBN-13: 9781662539343 (hardcover)
ISBN-13: 9781662537660 (paperback)
ISBN-13: 9781662537677 (digital)

Cover design by Emily Mahar
Cover Image © photocreo.com / Alamy; © Yuriy Kotsulym / Getty

Printed in the United States of America
First edition

*For Natalie Corinne.
To the moon and back, kid.*

The doors of hell are locked on the inside.
—C. S. Lewis

Chapter 1

Soon

Rubbing his hands against the cold, the deliveryman stands on their porch, facing them through the open front door. Hipster beard, gauge earrings, knit cap. Given what he is delivering, he seems so ordinary. Rebecca wonders if he has any idea.

She decides his name is Joe. Delivery Joe. He likes craft beer and grunge rock and smokes indica on weekends.

Mark is at her back. She eases into him. He puts his arms around her.

The forms Rebecca must sign to take possession are elaborate, pages of legalese she pretends to read on the electronic pad. They'd already been over the terms extensively with their euphemistically named "Experience Facilitator" on the video teleconference. The woman was severely pretty, scraped-back ice-blond hair, Scandinavian cheekbones, faint accent of indeterminate origin. Her bloodred lipstick, like the rest of her, straight out of Hitchcock. Her name was Luca, or so they'd been told. She'd been assigned to them for the process, which so far has felt bespoke and vaguely contrived.

Rebecca's gaze lifts to this object that she and Mark have invited into their house, into their lives.

Resting atop a futuristic dolly beside Delivery Joe, it is coffin-large, crated in wood, like something that came over on a merchant ship in the 1800s.

Delivery Joe's breath huffs in the air like cigarette smoke. The van behind him is sleek, windowless, without a logo. His gloved hand grips the dolly handle.

Rebecca realizes she has stiffened in Mark's arms.

"Something wrong, Mrs. Higgins?" Delivery Joe asks.

She isn't sure what he means. Then he chins at the electronic pad, and she comes back into herself, the stylus poised above the touch screen.

They can still refuse delivery.

Now is their last chance.

But then what? Back to their routine with its familiar contours and repetitive challenges? Life bled dry of unpredictability? The stifling gray smog of caretaker fatigue and unresolved grief?

They are in their early forties, but it feels already that they know the shape of everything to come.

Behind them, Maddy wanders through the foyer, singing absentmindedly to herself, wearing her ballet tights and tutu she has refused to take off since her recital last week. She hugs Bao-Bao, their six-pound Mini Lop bunny, around his midsection, his front legs scrunched upward in a painful-looking shrug, his lower half dangling to her knees. His nose twitches. He is used to these aggressive bouts of love.

The sight of Maddy breaks Rebecca from her trance. She signs.

Mark, too, snaps into motion, unlatching the flush bolts on the fixed half of the front doors, swinging both wide to accommodate the load.

Maddy has paused, staring through the gaping front doors at this thing they are going to allow across the threshold of their house.

"What's that, Mommy?" Her face is twisted in an adorable display of curiosity, a little furl on her forehead. How pure emotions are in seven-year-olds. They feel what they are feeling all the time in real time. Even more so when they are "on the spectrum," a phrase Rebecca hates for its overuse and lack of human specificity.

How long has it been since Rebecca felt with that much purity?

"Take Bao-Bao to your room, Maddysaurus. We'll explain later."

Maddy withdraws like the good, good girl she is.

Delivery Joe takes back the pad, scrolls through it, making sure Rebecca has initialed all the boxes. He is chewing nicotine gum. Smelling the tobacco tang on his breath brings her back to undergraduate nights out in Boston with Mark, how they used to social-smoke and drink black and tans in the pubs by Fenway, how they'd make out on the T, heading back to campus. It had felt so free, every night a seed for a different future.

"M'kay," Delivery Joe says, still checking. And then, "M'kay, m'kay. We're good. You ordered the white-glove delivery but—" He holds up his hands. His gloves are black. He emits a chunk of a laugh, mirthless. "Try not to read into it."

Mark says, "We won't take it personally."

"As your Experience Facilitator should've informed you, 's gonna require a Level 2 setup, 240-volt power source, dedicated charging point."

Luca had indeed covered this as well. Once a shipping update had made the whole enterprise suddenly concrete last month, they'd had a Tesla Supercharger installed.

"Remember," Delivery Joe says, with a practiced lilt of repetition that feels decidedly theatrical, like everything else related to the endeavor, "you're in charge."

He presses a button on the dolly. It's an elaborate modern contraption that raises itself up, wheels adjusting robotically like the treads of a tank, preparing to crawl across the threshold just as it crawled up the front steps. Those tiny, hard wheels remind her of shark teeth, infinitely layered.

The dolly and its load hover, poised to enter.

"Where d'ya want it?" he asks.

Behind her, Rebecca hears Maddy's bedroom door click shut. The autumn breeze blows roughly across her face, bringing up blood in her cheeks.

She looks to Mark. He hesitates too.

"The nursery," he says.

It is still painted a beautiful blue, though the crib is gone, as well as the optimistic teddy bear, also blue, and the changing table. It's been eleven months since the miscarriage, but it feels like minutes. They'd had fertility issues before, and the doctor said there's no more trying now, but that's okay because they have Maddy, and Maddy is perfect.

Nudged to life, the dolly gives a mechanical whir and progresses toward the laid-open front doors of their home.

They have to step aside to make way.

Chapter 2

Nine Months Before Delivery

It is their first night out since the horror-movie nightmare in the bathroom, red-brown spatter on the matte porcelain floor tiles, Rebecca curled up against the bathtub, sobbing, Mark at a loss, Maddy in the doorway, stimming, the whole house, their whole life, wildly dysregulated.

Rebecca is wearing a little black dress and heels, and it's been so long since she's applied makeup that she can feel it on her face. Putting herself together to go out felt mournful and exhausting, but this is what she needs to do as a woman and a wife and a mother and a person who is still alive.

Mark looks sharp in his Ralph Lauren pants and tailored black blazer. They have always been comfortable but are new to having real money. Since the e-news content optimization company Mark works for went public last year, they are spending more freely but are still at the stage where they remember how much everything costs: the aforementioned slacks, her Kate Spade wristlet, their staggeringly overpriced 2,500-square-foot Brentwood house.

They are at the Beverly Hills Hotel's Polo Lounge for cocktails, and Rebecca has already made the requisite joke about Mark's pants matching the environment, and they've ordered the fancy-pants cocktails they can suddenly afford, and the lull has now arrived, the lonely black space of their loss in the midst of all the laughter and tinkling of silverware and piano keys.

At booths and tables all around them, confidence is on peacock display. Dagger slits in sequined dresses. Hollywood agent types in slick suits, mouths rat-a-tatting like machine guns. Well-padded European men luxuriating in velour casual wear, slurping oysters with second wives who are indiscernible from high-class call girls.

It comes on first as heat beneath the bridge of her nose and a quiver in her throat, and then Rebecca is crying quietly. She dabs at her eyes with the black linen napkin the waiter had produced for her to preempt unseemly white lint against her dress.

"I'm sorry," she says quietly. "I'm sorry."

Mark rubs the back of her neck. His eyes are pouched from lack of sleep. He looks far wearier than his forty-two years, and she feels that this, like everything else, is her fault.

She lowers her face as their drinks arrive in a flourish to sit untouched on the cocktail table before them.

Mark lowers his hand, and they sit side by side, unsure what to say. The whole outing feels at once carnival-foolish. They marinate for a minute in regret over their choice of environment, and then he says, "Maybe we should get the check?"

"Okay, yeah," Rebecca says, fumbling out her phone. "And I just want to check on Maddy."

Maddy is with her favorite babysitter, and she doesn't need checking, but Rebecca cannot help it. Once you realize that you live in a world where a baby can die inside your body, everything feels unsafe. When their little family of three was on its way to becoming a quartet, the future seemed unbounded, safe, full of hope. Now tomorrow feels thwarted and every tomorrow and tomorrow and tomorrow after that.

"She's fine," Mark says. "It's good for her to go an evening without touching base."

Rebecca cradles her phone, the number of Maddy's emergency cell already called up on the screen, tempting. She knows that the urge to call is for herself, not for Maddy. She knows, too, that it won't allay her anxiety; it'll just ingrain the habit of checking-checking-checking. And that she is transferring her grief over the miscarriage into concern about her living child, which is unfair to Maddy and stultifying for herself. If only *understanding* something could alleviate the underlying compulsion. But no,

Rebecca is aware and incapable at the same time. Is she becoming the Devouring Mother she studied in cultural anthropology in college, so desperate to shield her vulnerable child that she'd rather swallow her up than sacrifice her to an uncaring world?

She goes for a half measure, calling up the teddy bear nanny-cam app. There Maddy is, frog-sitting on the foam tiles in her bedroom, wearing her noise-canceling headphones and finishing her Lego giraffe. Babysitter June lies on Maddy's bed with her legs up the wall and her head dangling backward off the mattress, watching her phone upside down. All quiet on the home front.

Rebecca slips her phone back inside the ridiculous pink wristlet that looked so fetching displayed on the underlit boutique shelf. Now it seems like a prop. Her stomach is a swirling black hole, eating itself from the inside. She thinks of Maddy's wide eyes, the way she cries after school when Sydney and the other Mean Girls play their Mean Girl games, how she never understands why she doesn't fit in, why kids revel in petty cruelties, why psychosomatic stomachaches land her with the school nurse three days of the week.

"What if . . . ?"

"What, Beccs?"

"What if I'd watched her food better? All organic or—I don't know—only farm to table? There's forever chemicals in every-thing—bottled water, plastic wrap. Hormones in the meat and chicken, milk and eggs. I could've done homemade baby food, spread out her vaccinations. It's like everything's trying to poison us, our kids. Big food, big tech, Big Pharma. Her meds—she's on so many meds, and meds for the side effects of her meds, and she's just a baby still, just seven, and maybe we—I don't know, I love her more than anything, and she's perfect, but what if . . ."

Mark's head inclines slightly in that graceful manner he has. "No," he says gently. "Maddy is Maddy. And thank God for that. We couldn't have done anything different. It's not your fault."

She swipes at her eyes angrily. Her mascara is no-run, a prophylactic measure she'd been wise to take. She knows she is spiraling, that she is not in real time, that grief is speaking through her, using her like a puppet. "I could've eaten better. And the beach, Santa Monica, the water quality . . ."

"We have to live in the world, Beccs. We live in the real world."

"We could've moved to the country or something, less toxins, pollutants." She is talking nonsense, but she cannot stop. Her hand has slid down to her stomach, and when she speaks again, her voice comes as a whisper: "What if I did something to cause this too?"

"Oh, Beccs. Oh, no, honey. No, no, no."

He leans to her, and she nuzzles into his neck. He smells like sage and cedar—the soap she bought for him on a day trip to Ojai—and for the thousandth time this week she thanks the universe for delivering him to her. Though they have plenty of blessings, she wants nothing more than a chance to rest, a break from her rabbiting mind. "I'm sorry."

"You have nothing to apologize for."

"But I'm all cry-y like I get. And we're supposed to be on a date."

"We're grieving, Beccs. This is what this date looks like." He reaches for his cocktail, a penicillin. The waft of peat reaching her nose smells like Band-Aids. He offers his glass in a toast. "One sip," he says, "and we'll call it a night."

Her gin and tonic fills a ridiculous balloon glass, augmented with sprigs and peppercorn. It looks like a witch's cauldron. They clink their glasses, sip, set them down.

Two tables over, a woman brays laughter, throwing back her head, vixen-red tresses parting to reveal a milk white throat. Her manicured fingertips trawl along her décolletage, drawing focus even in Rebecca's peripheral vision.

Rebecca feels frumpy and ordinary, a child playing dress-up. She cannot wait to leave here, to be home in bed in her jammies, lying on Mark's chest.

He gestures for the check.

"Mark?"

Rebecca's stomach clutches.

The woman has called over to their table.

That voice, velvety and familiar.

"Mark and Rebecca?"

The squeak of chairs shoving out, a couple rising. Rebecca feels that heat again beneath her face and for a terrible instant thinks she might just break down and start sobbing.

Alexa de Grasse. And her husband, Derek, Mark's big boss.

At the holiday party last year at Soho House, Alexa drank too many cosmos and tried to make out with Mark on the rooftop garden in front of half the marketing department.

Though Derek brushed the incident off, covering with aggressive affability, he has never forgiven Mark for it. Given that Derek is the founder, CEO, and self-proclaimed visionary, while Mark is one of three chief product officers clinging to the C-suite by their fingernails, that adds an undertow to an already-strained dynamic.

And now here they are, the de Grasses, pulling up chairs to their table. The pianist has taken a break from the sleek Steinway grand, and the semisilence feels intrusive, an acoustic spotlight glare fixed on their table.

"Well, well, well," Derek says, grinning big as he sinks into his seat. "Look who the cat dragged in."

Alexa descends into a chair with a balletic swing of hips, fold of legs, tuck of hem beneath the thighs. Her champagne flute, narrow like her waist, effervesces. Her cheeks are flushed, her eyes a touch wild. It is not her first glass.

"Surprising to see you two here," Alexa says in something of a purr. Her bitter perfume is less an aroma than a flick to the nose.

"Oh?" Mark says, "Why's that?"

"It's not a *bad* thing. Just, you two always struck me more as homebody types."

"Not far off the mark," Rebecca says, leaning in. "In fact, we were just—"

"C'mon. It's Saturday night, and the mood is right." Derek signals the waiter, arm shooting up, fingers just shy of a snap.

Saturday night, sure, but Sunday is Rebecca's chore day—laundry and grocery shopping, making lunch, cleaning Bao-Bao's cage, coordinating pickups and drop-offs and appointments, preparing for the week. She wishes that she could clone herself, that there were two of her to perform the daily tasks that suck away all her hours, tasks that shouldn't feel nearly as draining as they do. Then she could have time to—time to what? Read on the sofa? Go to a matinee? Finally call her estranged mother? Something, anything to reclaim that full-of-life college girl she seems to have lost somewhere along the way.

Derek squeezes the back of Mark's neck, a dude-bro clench that's a touch too hard. "Glad you're enjoying your weekend nights while you have 'em," he says. "Once we start updating the customer-service modules, you'll be sleeping on your desk blotter."

"AI chatbots," Mark says. "What could go wrong?"

The waiter materializes at Derek's elbow. "A second round of everything," Derek proclaims grandly. "And port my tab over here. I'll cover all this."

"That's not necessary," Mark says.

"And we're good," Rebecca says. "We just started on these."

"It's okay," Derek confides in the waiter. "They'll catch up."

His credit card rises between two fingers. The waiter pockets it with grace and withdraws.

Rebecca feels Alexa's eyes picking over her. Derek leans to the side, examines Mark's outfit. "Nice pants," he says. "Purple Label?"

"Thanks," Mark says. "Second time I've put 'em on. I'm still amortizing them."

Rebecca and Mark did well with their stock options, but Derek did spectacularly. He has a stunt plane and a private jet in a hangar in Santa Monica and restores antique Porsches in his spare time. The de Grasses have a passel of children, four or five—Rebecca has lost count.

"Isn't that the dress you wore to the holiday party?" Alexa says. And then quickly: "I like it. It's . . . *cute*."

Rebecca shrugs. "I don't remember. Probably."

"I don't remember much from that party either." Alexa laughs, and Derek stiffens slightly, an inadvertent show of unease. "When I drink too much—*wooo*!" Her hands fly up, and sparkly bracelets slide down her forearms, glimmering. She is wearing gold metallic gladiator heels, straps wrapping her calves, snakelike. They look like sexy garters for the feet. "Anyhoo, we've all been there." She reaches those manicured nails for her husband's cheek, smooths a lock of hair back around his ear. Her eyes, an improbable contact-lens emerald, find Rebecca's. "Sorry to just flutter over here. Y'all looked so serious. What did we bust in on?"

"We were just talking about getting back to Maddy."

"Ah." Alexa lays her hand on Rebecca's forearm, eyes intense with performative concern. "How *is* she?"

"Great," Mark says curtly. "She's great."

"Good," Alexa says. "That's so good. She's such a dear."

"We sent ours off to boarding school," Derek says. "New Hampshire. All four of them."

"Derek's alma mater. The house is *so quiet*."

"But we love it."

Alexa puts her hand to the side of her mouth, leans in to stage-whisper: "So much time to fight or fuck."

Rebecca and Mark don't fight or fuck very often anymore.

Their schedule is filled with hard work, parenting, recovery.

"Don't you miss them?" Rebecca asks.

"Well, the academy sends us these once a week," Alexa says, producing her phone and flicking through photos, her pointer finger bent to meet the screen with her print, the nail flared back. Something about the toggling gesture feels suggestive. She shows Rebecca several photos of their children, indistinguishably attractive and healthy, performing various athletic and scholarly feats. "Proof of life."

"Gives me more garage time," Derek says. "You should see the Targa I just got at auction, a 997.2 4S."

"He outbid Jerry Seinfeld *and* Jay Leno."

"But we get the kids for Thanksgiving, Christmas, ski week, all summer," Derek adds quickly. "It's good for them to get instruction elsewhere too. It was good for me."

"I don't know what we'd do with all that time," Rebecca says.

"Oh, we figured out what to do," Alexa says wickedly. Her eyes flash to her husband. "Should we share?"

Derek bites back a grin, gives a flirtatious single shoulder shrug.

Alexa turns to Rebecca, hands clasping her hand on the table, the kind of girlfriend-y clasp Rebecca never sees deployed outside of movies. "Do you want to know? Do you *really* want to know?"

Rebecca says, "Sure," because there is no other answer to give.

The waiter returns, his tray brimming with drinks, and a conspiratorial hush falls over the table. Whatever the de Grasses have to share is not for just anyone's ears.

Derek and Alexa study each other dramatically. "Are you sure?" he asks.

"Of course," Alexa breathes. "They need it." And then reassuringly: "We needed it too."

Derek takes out his wallet contraption, a stubby metal rectangle with buttons. Only Derek would have a mechanized wallet, likely something exotically Kickstarted by some life hack engineer in Bengaluru. He pushes a button and a titanium business card pops free of the wallet as if from a toaster, a cheap magician's trick.

"This," he says grandly, "this is our plus-one."

He displays the card.

It says: **N0RM LLC**.

There is a website, an email, a 1-800 number.

"Started by a South African technocrat." Derek's teeth are very shiny. So is his hair. He is handsome, too handsome to be attractive, strong of jaw, sculpted from marble. "A no-shit genius. I met him in Sun Valley, one of those thought-leader summits."

"*Very* exclusive," Alexa says. "The company's clientele, I mean. Not the Sun Valley borefest."

Rebecca takes the card, fingers the corner, testing it like the tip of a blade.

"Turn it over," Derek says.

Stamped on the back: **YOU'RE IN CHARGE**.

"We got in on the beta stage," Derek says. "It's extremely limited availability, but we're allowed to pass on the offer to one other party."

Mark asks, "What is it?"

"It's a dream," Derek says. "No—a fantasy."

"Like . . ." Alexa contemplates, front teeth pinching a collagen-stung lower lip, crystalline green eyes tugged upward, a perfect selfie pose. "The ultimate retail therapy."

Rebecca sets the card down on the table with a metallic click. "Perhaps some more specificity."

Instantly she regrets the irritation she's let leak into her tone, but the de Grasses do not take notice, at last a benefit of their self-centeredness.

Derek swirls his scotch, allows a theatrical pause. "What if you could have something that knows everything about you, everything you want, and could get it for you? While staying totally under your control?"

Alexa's voice is seductive and slightly crass: "Let's just say it's designed for your gratification. It'll see to everything you *really* want. In your darkest heart of hearts." She rests a scarlet fingernail on the card, slides it across to Mark, and then leans close to Rebecca, her breath tasting of alcohol and perhaps a bygone cigarette. "This? This will change *everything*."

Rebecca closes her eyes. Feels a phantom pulse of pain in her lower abdomen, across her back. Sees the crimson handprint she left when she gripped the side of the bathtub. Thinks about school drop-offs, visits with the nurse, the occupational therapist, the psychiatrist for Maddy. Feels the sorrow like lead in her bone marrow, the grief she drags through her days. She is much too young to feel so exhausted, so leached of optimism.

More than anything she feels *stuck*, her wheels churning in ever-deepening ruts. No one ever taught her this, how torpor can be more oppressive than grief, a lead apron that pins you down, makes you want to quit struggling and just give up. And she hates to admit—*hates* to admit—that dealing with Maddy and her special needs takes so much out of her. Is the apple sauce too chunky? Are the lights too bright in the bank lobby? Are her stuffties out of order on the shelf? She's just one kid, one sweet, lovely kid, and yet at the end of most days, Rebecca's nervous system feels shorted out from hypervigilance.

She doesn't like to see herself as desperate and yet here she is, barely treading water for herself and her little family, and here Derek and Alexa are, too, tossing her a lifeline. She thinks about the allure of control and the promise of change, gift horses and mouths, beggars and choosers. A thunderstorm of metaphors for the bare, naked fact that she would give anything—*anything*—just to feel different.

When she opens her eyes, Mark is looking at her, his gaze shiny with interest. He gives a hint of a one-shoulder shrug.

Rebecca picks up the card again.

And says, "Tell me more."

Chapter 3

Rebecca is where she wanted to be, burrowed into the sheets, lying on Mark's chest, but now she realizes that she doesn't want to be here at all. She doesn't want to be anywhere.

Maddy's nigh-night routine was elaborate as always, an hour-long ritual—bath, soap, shampoo, dry, lotion, brush hair, brush teeth, pee, princess nightgown, goodnight kisses to Bao-Bao in his crate in the kitchen, *sleep tight* hugs to all the stuffties on the shelf—Mr. Elephant, Mr. Pig, Mr. Caterpillar, et cetera—fluff pillows, tuck blankets to the chin; *Horton Hears a Who!*; *Good Night, Gorilla*; *Goodnight Moon*; sleep-inducing nose pets, Sleeptime Pillow Pet that casts stars on the ceiling, count the stars, make the wishes, nighttime affirmations—*My voice matters. I tried my best today. I am still growing and learning. I have what it takes*—forehead kiss, sneak out of the room, two minutes of peace, glass-of-water request, repeat process from affirmations onward.

The **N0RM LLC** business card beckons from Mark's nightstand, glinting in the light of the alarm. Had the Polo Lounge discussion with Alexa and Derek actually happened? Could something like that possibly be real? The de Grasses had been vague and coy with their answers about what *precisely* to expect, which felt manipulative and on brand for them. But the mysteriousness also made the opportunity—though this is hard for Rebecca to admit—enticing.

Her iPhone is turned off, but the silence is not blissful. It shouts that she is missing things, falling desperately behind. Snippets of the evening's conversation with Alexa and Derek rush to fill the quiet of her mind.

The surprise is part of it. The sense of adventure.

You'll see.

Pricey but well worth it. Two hundred twenty-five K all in.

An investment!

Think of it this way: What's money for, if not this?

It is insane. Insane and out of the question for her and Mark and their normal life.

She is too tired to sleep. Her stomach roils, a match for her mind. She can feel Mark humming beside her as well, electricity moving through the warm skin of his chest into her cheek.

"What's with his jawline?" she says.

Mark will know she means Derek. They have it like that, shorthand and shared jokes, swimming inside a shared stream of consciousness.

"I believe he had it surgically enhanced," Mark says.

"Augmented with panda bone."

"At a *very exclusive* medical facility in Dubai."

"The Buzz Lightyear Special."

It feels good to smile. He runs his fingertips across her shoulders. Even through her stretched-out Tufts T-shirt, it feels good.

A thought niggles at the base of her brain. "Do you find her attractive?"

Her face rises and falls with Mark's breaths. He is taking longer to answer than she would like.

"In an ice-queen way, I suppose," he says.

The answer is a needle jab to her heart. She knows that her reaction is petty. But she also feels . . . How does she feel? Washed out? Less than?

She is silent. Mark breathes some more.

She lifts her head and looks up at his shadowed face. The titanium business card winks at her from the nightstand. A dozen insecure responses rise in her throat, and she sets them down one after another.

"Good night," she says.

"'Night, Beccs."

She slides off him, rolls over, nerves jangling inside her. And hormones. The doctor told her that her progesterone and estrogen would take weeks to stabilize, and here she is two months later, filled with typhoons and tornadoes, bobbing like a cork on a tidal wave. How easy it is to forget that we are all just mammals.

She wants to weep. She wants to scream. She wants to be herself again, her stable, adult self.

She does not want to cry. Mark will feel awful, and he doesn't need to carry any more than he is already gracefully carrying. A feeling beckons, dark and yet delicious, that he deserves more than this. That *they* deserve more than this.

Which is precisely what N0RM LLC claims to offer.

Mark's breathing is steady. He is asleep already, and she is alone.

But then he says, "I can't imagine sleeping next to her. So, no, I can't imagine sleeping *with* her. She doesn't have your heart, Beccs. No one does."

Warmth moves through her entire body, a surge of oxytocin. She wriggles backward toward him, shoves her hind quarters into his side. He loops his arm beneath her neck, and they fall asleep together in the shared heat of their bodies.

Chapter 4

The Night of Delivery

Rebecca stands in the doorway of the nursery, the futuristic object looking incongruous, centered there on its base within the baby blue walls. A rectangular prism with rounded corners, recessed lights, and a clamshell lid, it resembles a closed tanning bed.

N0RM LLC is laser etched right there on the side. The sensor light just above it glows red.

The power cable is connected to the charging point. An inset touch screen on the side has allowed for interface with their wireless network, granting access to their computers, search histories, calendars, online shopping patterns, cell phones, vehicular GPSs, smart appliances, wearable devices, and the far-field microphones embedded in all their technologies that allow for hands-free and voice recognition.

Soon it will know them better than they know themselves.

And that is the point.

Because then it can see to their wishes.

It is a relief to know that relief is coming.

And yet something has prompted Rebecca to rise now, at the edge of midnight, to lean against the doorjamb and observe this contraption they have invited into their home. Her arms are crossed against the cold, but still she shudders.

The rectangular prism vibrates and hums gently.

Something growing within.

What precisely it is, they have no idea. That is part of the fun, part of the adventure, part of the torment.

"Beccs?"

She starts, gives a yelp.

Mark puts his arms around her, pulls her in. "It's me," he says. "It's just me."

"You scared the bejesus out of me."

"What *is* a bejesus precisely?" Mark asks.

"And why do we only take note when it's scared out of us?" she mumbles into his chest.

He runs his fingers soothingly through her hair. "Valid," he says. "Folks rarely note that they're walking around contently filled with bejesus."

"Either way," she says, "it's out of me, the bejesus, and you are to blame."

They rock a bit in each other's arms. She senses that, like her, he is equal parts excited and apprehensive. They know some of what to expect. But something like this cannot be fully anticipated any more than a child. Or a miscarriage.

It just has to get here, and then they will try to make sense of what they paid so much for.

"This'll be good, right?" she says.

Mark is quiet for a moment, and then she feels him nodding.

Past his shoulder she sees the rectangular prism glowing, right in the spot where the crib used to be.

Chapter 5

Eight Months Before Delivery

The titanium business card has vanished into Mark's nightstand drawer, out of view and somewhat out of mind, though Rebecca thinks of it more often than she wants to admit. The notion remains alluring. And given the success of Mark's company, they did have $225,000, not necessarily to spare, but to spend wisely on something they wouldn't regret. That would burn about two years of their mortgage runway, diminishing their fund by half, but given Mark's salary and the stock performance, they could replenish in time without taking a lifestyle hit.

The daily grind keeps grinding, her cell phone dinging constantly with notifications and updates, a slot machine singing its dark siren song. In response to bullying at school, Maddy's hand-flapping has flared up again, straining her tendons and fatiguing her wrist muscles, so now she is wearing forearm braces, which invites more bullying. This has led to a spate of additional appointments—ortho, therapist, school nurse, teacher, principal—in addition to the other tasks of Westside living. A broken solar panel results in five phone calls and three rescheduled appointments. A volunteer shortage at kiss-and-ride drop-off at the elementary school requires Rebecca to pick up two more shifts a week; the school does so much to accommodate Maddy that she always wants to be the first to answer an ask for help. All this has been negotiated with painstaking inefficiency over text and email in threads and subthreads.

On top of this, she's working hard to find healthy food that takes less prep time, running through Trader Joe's to grab premade meals, frozen entrées, and prechopped celery and carrots.

Now she is racing home from her oft-delayed OB/GYN follow-up so she can prep dinner before Maddy's after-school pickup, free Bao-Bao from his crate, and wait the inexplicable four-hour window required by the HVAC guy. Lurching through traffic, she tries Mark.

As usual these days, he sounds harried when he picks up. "You good?"

"Yep," she says. "Just wanted to hear your voice."

"Aw. Nice to hear yours." Mark drops his register. "Derek's been on the warpath leading up to quarterlies. I have a Zoom in—shit—two minutes ago. Can I . . ."

"Go. See you tonight."

"I'll try to get there to do Maddy's nigh-night wind-down. But I'm not sure . . ."

"It's okay. I got it. I'll save you a plate."

"Thank you, ÜberWife."

"You're welcome, ÜberHusband."

When she disconnects the call, she feels a surge of sadness and has to tell herself not to come apart. Why? How did she get this fragile? How can life possibly feel this challenging here in affluent Brentwood?

Their neighbor Jackson is up on a ladder fussing with his rain gutters. His black BMW sits beneath his carport, polished as always, the license plate frame broadcasting his USC fraternity. As she pulls into her driveway, he hops down and comes flying through the muddy break in the hedge. A mortgage salesman in his late twenties, he is an unremitting asshole.

Rebecca avoids him at all costs.

"The *fuck*, Rebecca," Jackson says as she gathers armfuls of grocery bags from the trunk of her Nissan Quest minivan. "Your fucking pine tree is still dropping shit onto my roof. I have sap in the gutter again and eating through the shingles."

"I'm sorry," Rebecca says, the apology out of her mouth before she can reel it in. "We had it trimmed. It's not over the property line anym—"

"Ever heard of *wind*, Rebecca? Breeze? I'm still getting debris all over my roof, clogging the drainpipes, gunking up my walkway. It's expensive as fuck to fix."

He is standing in her driveway, staring in at her in the garage. She wants to ask him to leave. Behind him the grand pine tree sways and bristles. Forked near the base, it pins down their patch of front lawn, a magnificent winged totem. She loves how unlikely it is here in Brentwood among the usual palms and oaks, the wintry scent of it, how the sun plays through the needles, texturing the air. In all its mess and glory, it was part of what first drew her to the house.

"Don't swear at me," she says meekly.

"Oh, *swearing's* the problem." Jackson waves his hands. "Sorry. Don't mean to be toxic while I'm busy cleaning up your mess. *Again.*"

"You can talk to Mark—"

"I'm sick of talking to Mark. Keep your waste product off my property or else—I have a buddy from college who's a big-time lawyer."

"There's nothing illegal about having trees, Jackson."

"Fine. Fine. Play it that way? I'll just poison the fucking thing."

Jackson stomps off.

She is shaken. He has threatened to kill something that she loves, and the brashness of it, the menace and meanness, strikes her somewhere deeper than words. Heading inside, she dumps the bags on the kitchen island and stands trembling for a moment. Why didn't she speak up? If anyone deserves to be frankly and fully told to fuck off, it is Jackson.

She certainly has the wit and bite. She could've mocked his inflated terms—*waste product, big-time lawyer*. She could've slapped him down with poised indignation. She could've ordered him to get off her property.

But she'd been intimidated. Maybe that's where Maddy got it, this excessive sensitivity, the surfeit of feeling, an inability to think clearly in the face of cruelty.

She puts the groceries away, feeds Bao-Bao a quarter cup of pellets, moves the laundry to the dryer. Then for the first time in two days she takes a shower.

She tries to awaken her body, but she feels numb.

Defeated, she climbs out, towels off, dresses. In the back of the small walk-in closet sit her half-finished canvases and folded-up easel, abandoned since she was in her third term with Maddy. They stare at her, a nagging rebuke for all the parts of herself she's been unable to keep up with.

She sits on the bed, takes a few breaths.

Her gaze moves to Mark's nightstand.

She slides over, opens the drawer. The titanium card glimmers up at her. **YOU'RE IN CHARGE.**

She takes it out.

Chapter 6

One Month After Delivery

It takes three cycles of Maddy's nigh-night routine before she stays down. Rebecca and Mark sit on the floor in the hall outside her closed door, listening for another request—water, bathroom, beneath-the-bed search.

But the silence stretches five minutes and then ten, and then by implicit agreement, they rise silently and creep down the hall to the nursery.

The hum of the rectangular prism has steadily grown louder. Code scrolls across the inset screen. It is as if they are watching something dream. As if they are peeking in on a sleeping baby.

They note the sensor light on the prism.

It remains red.

They withdraw.

Chapter 7

Seven Months Before Delivery

The kit has arrived.

Now it is real.

Rebecca still can't believe that they did it.

The payment phase has not been without complication. The day after the wire for the $75,000 nonretrievable downpayment cleared, Mark's company missed its quarterly earnings estimates, the stock taking a tumble. They'd debated mightily whether to cut their losses, to not throw good money after bad. But they've already paid 33 percent of the total, and giving up on what still felt like the chance of a lifetime to "change *everything*" seems a shame. On top of that, Derek has gotten more demanding of Mark at the office, asking him to work longer and longer hours, and Maddy has been spiraling at school.

They are sludging through darkness, the promise of N0RM LLC the light at the end of the tunnel.

They sit at the kitchen table, all three of them, four if you include Bao-Bao slumped in Maddy's lap. About the size of a toaster oven, the kit arrived special delivery, requiring signature at the door.

Mark slides the Styrofoam block out of the cube of a DHL Medical Express box. When he parts the block, dry ice mist leaks out, spilling across uncleared cereal bowls and OJ glasses, creeping to the edges of the table.

Bao-Bao's nose twitches mightily, and Maddy says, "Wowwowwow!"

Mark's hand disappears into the pool of mist and emerges holding several sterile pouches. He reads the instructions carefully, chewing his lip.

"What is it, Daddy?" Maddy asks. "What's it for?"

Rebecca answers for him before she can catch herself. "It's a surprise, honey."

"What kind of surprise?"

"It's going to help us," Mark says, tearing the lip off the first pouch and removing a long cotton swab.

"How?"

"We're not sure, Maddysaurus. I guess . . . I guess part of its job is to figure out what kind of help we need."

Maddy's face contorts in a scowl.

"Think of it like an adventure," Rebecca says, hating herself for parroting Alexa.

Mark considers the swab, shrugs, and then swabs his inner cheek with it, rubbing in a circular motion.

"Gross, Daddy!"

"Whath grosth?" Mark says, bugging out his eyes. "Thwy you fthink thuth ith grosth?"

Maddy's laugh is pure music.

Mark keeps on with the vaudeville bit as he does the other cheek, Maddy giggling uncontrollably. He is a wonderful father.

Then he waves the swab around like a wand, letting it air dry, the swirling mist augmenting the magic trick. "I choooooose . . . Mommy to go next." He points his swab-wand at Rebecca before sealing it in the collection tube.

She goes next.

"Make funny noises, Mommy," Maddy says, eyes brimming with her smile.

Rebecca does her best, but she is never as funny as Mark. Still, they laugh along with her.

Next up is Maddy.

She hesitates. "I want Bao-Bao to go instead."

"It's not for Bao-Bao," Mark says. "It's only for human family members."

As if on cue, Bao-Bao goes boneless and drools out of Maddy's lap. Maddy crosses her arms. With a flare of concern, Rebecca recognizes that expression. They have to leave for school soon and cannot afford a meltdown.

"Tell you what," Mark says quickly. "I'll swab for you, and *I'll* make the noises while we do it."

The scowl doesn't lift, but Maddy gives the faintest nod.

Once the swab goes into her mouth, Mark starts up the lisping and sputtering and Maddy laughs and laughs and then it is done.

Mark places all three collection tubes back into the Styrofoam block. Next he takes out a pair of insulated cryogenic gloves, so labeled on the plastic pouch, and dons them. Carefully, he frees a set of dry ice pellets from a metallic purse and pours them over the tubes.

Vapor plumes up as if from a cauldron, and Mark does Evil Plotting Fingers for Maddy before squeaking the Styrofoam top back onto the block.

He slides it into the DHL Express box, peels off the old label, and sticks on the new one that came with the shipment. A bit of packing tape, and it is done.

All three samples, neatly sealed inside.

Mark scans the barcode on the label with his phone, receives a satisfying ding. "We just leave it on the porch in the shade," he says, rising and grabbing his briefcase. "They'll pick it up within the hour."

Rebecca carries it outside, this precious package filled with their precious DNA. It seems odd to just leave it there beneath the porch swing, but that's what the instructions say to do.

They clear dishes, wipe counters. Rebecca loads Maddy's lunch into her stegosaurus lunch box. Corralling Bao-Bao into his crate takes some doing, and then they head to the garage together, Mark climbing in his venerable Lexus, Rebecca loading Maddy into the minivan booster seat, careful not to pinch her thigh with the seat belt and set off an escalation.

She slides the van door closed and comes around to Mark as he backs out into the driveway. He rolls down the window, and she leans on the sill with both arms to give him a kiss, their morning ritual.

Behind them, a DHL Express van rolls up to their house. She and Mark pause to watch the retrieval. A delivery gal hops out, jogs up the sidewalk, key clip jangling at her hip. She snatches up the box, jogs back, and the van is gone in a whir of tires.

Unease pulses to life inside Rebecca's stomach.

"That was fast," she says.

Shadows from the pine branches play across Mark's face. "Too late to turn back now."

The smile he cracks looks more nervous than amused.

Chapter 8

Two Months After Delivery

Maddy is crying in her room, sensory overload from the leaf blower and power mower roaring next door. The city has issued a ban on gas-powered landscaping tools, but Jackson and his gardeners don't care and Rebecca can't be bothered to confront him with everything else she has going on. At least that's what she is telling herself rather than admitting that she is scared of him and wants to avoid conflict. For the past half hour she's been running back and forth between Maddy and the laundry, and now she hears the teakettle she forgot about starting to scream; she'd promised Maddy Nervous Tummy Tea to calm her down.

Basket of whites on her hip, Rebecca races down the hall past the open nursery door. She is two steps from the kitchen when she registers what she observed.

The laundry basket hits the floor.

The teakettle pierces the air, vibrates the house. She hears a thumping from Maddy's room and prays she is not banging her head against the wall again.

For a moment she cannot move. The teakettle shrieks along with Maddy, but Rebecca remains frozen there a few strides past the nursery.

She eases back a step.

Another.

Peers inside.

Sure enough, the sensor light above the **N0RM LLC** laser etching has gone from red to green.

Chapter 9

Mark and Rebecca stand somberly over the rectangular prism. Aside from a ceramic moon night-light, the glow of the touch screen, and the green sensor dot, the nursery is dark. Next door Jackson is having a party, his stereo blaring so loud they had to turn up the volume on Maddy's sound soother. Evidently for Jackson, noise pollution isn't nearly as intrusive as having pine needles blown onto his property.

Everything feels scary—the coffin-like prism, the Gothic lighting, the thunder rumble of bass from next door. They observe silently, but there is no thunder from the heavens, no shifting of tectonic plates. Rebecca blows out a breath she didn't know she was holding, and Mark follows suit. They laugh a little at themselves.

She is tempted to lift the prism's lid, but there is no handle, no latch, the seam so tight that not even fingernails can slip in to pry it up.

It only opens from the inside.

"What do we do?" Mark asks.

"I guess wait," Rebecca says.

Her answer hangs heavily in the air between them. Mark doesn't seem to like it any more than she does.

Chapter 10

They awaken to the sound of running water coming from somewhere down the hall. Is it a leak? An intruder? Could that be the shower?

Rebecca jerks up, wild eyed. Mark is already shoving his legs into jeans.

She thinks of the busted pipe they had last winter that flooded the powder room and forced them to tear out the floor and redo the wainscoting.

A flicker in a dark corner of her mind conjures up the rectangular prism, but she is not willing to contend with the notion in full at 2:37 in the morning.

She pulls on a bathrobe and enters the hall at Mark's back. Maddy's door is closed. The nursery door too.

They creep down the unlit hall together in the direction of the kitchen. As they near the nursery, it becomes undeniable that the sound of rushing water is issuing from behind the shut door.

Rebecca's breath has quickened, shallow gasps. Her vision starts to dot, and she reminds herself to draw full inhalations. Ever the stalwart engineer, Mark proceeds, steady on his feet.

His hand on the doorknob, he hesitates. Looks back at Rebecca.

She gives him a quick downward jerk of her chin, the best version of a nod she can muster.

He twists the knob.

The door opens with a faint squeak of hinges.

It takes a moment for them to comprehend what they are seeing.

The lid of the prism is lifted.

The inside, shadowed.

Spots glimmer wetly on the floor.

Puddles?

No—footprints.

The marks of bare feet, outlined in translucent goo.

The footsteps lead across the laminate floorboards to the bathroom. The door is slightly ajar, steam from the shower sheeting through the gap.

Mark breathes more than speaks: "What the actual fuck?"

She has never heard his voice this way. She tries to respond but cannot.

They draw close to the open prism, peering over the lip, holding their weight back on their heels as if they are gazing over the edge of a cliff.

The first thing Rebecca notices is the bed of goo, viscous and clear. It reminds her of the ultrasound gel applied liberally across her pregnant belly, the primordial sludge that accompanies the emergence of life. The bed is indented in the middle, like a body impression on a well-used mattress. The goo is lit a futuristic blue from beneath and both sides by what look to be microchips lining the casket's interior.

"Circuit boards?" Mark says in that same breathless voice.

Once again they track the trail of footprints leading to the bathroom.

Rebecca can't help but notice the heavy-handed stagecraft of steam turning the room into a science fiction landscape. Without dropping her eyes from that gap in the door, she reaches for Mark's hand, which finds hers halfway between them.

His palm feels cool against hers, which has gone clammy with fright.

They stand there frozen, unsure.

And then the shower shuts off.

Then comes the purr of the shower door rolling back on its modern-by-way-of-Restoration-Hardware barn track. It thuds to a stop.

Rebecca's ears are suddenly and acutely attuned. She can hear the sound of water dripping onto the bath mat. The whoosh of a towel pulled smoothly from the rack. Fibers drawn across . . . skin? The pad of a footstep. Another.

And then the bathroom door inches outward.

A form stares there in the doorframe, backlit and naked, bath sheet hanging from one hand at its side.

For a moment, Rebecca thinks it is Mark.

"Hello," it says.

Rebecca's throat is too dry to use.

It steps forward into the light. Smooth features, average build. It—he?—is well endowed but not grotesquely so. The only thing grotesque is the flagrant sight of his nakedness. His parts seem nonoperational, statuesque, in the image of man rather than man himself. He is not bald so much as hairless. Smooth limbs, no eyelashes, twinning ridges of—flesh? latex?—above each eye in place of brows.

Somehow in the midst of all this, Rebecca finds time to marvel that the grayish shade of his skin seems engineered to inoculate against any sensitive issues around race.

The form-thing-man gets down on all fours and begins mopping up the goo footprints with the bath towel. "Don't worry," he says, "this will wash out of the bath sheet." His voice is flat but not robot flat; there is a soothing human inflection to it. "What would you like to call me?"

Mark and Rebecca exchange an anxious glance.

Mark manages to respond: "I . . . don't know."

"I will wear clothing for your and Maddy's comfort," the thing-man says. "I fit the same size of clothes that Mark wears. The T-shirt pack you bought at Costco last week is fine. Same with the sweatpants you ordered from Amazon and a pair of the 501s purchased on June 13 from Levi.com."

Mark manages to say "Right." He clears his throat and clears it again. "How about . . . footwear?"

"I don't wear shoes. Being barefoot provides better sensory input for balance and coordination."

Mark nods several times rapidly, processing, and then takes a step toward the door.

Rebecca grabs his arm. "I'll get the clothes. Why don't you wait here." It is not a question.

Moving swiftly, she fetches the items, rushing between rooms, breath hammering in her throat.

When she returns, Mark is precisely where she left him. The thing-man is standing, the sodden towel neatly folded at his feet along with two others from the bathroom.

"I can put this in the laundry," he says as he gets dressed. "I'll do colors and whites tomorrow so the dryer won't wake Maddy up."

"Mommy?"

Maddy stands in the doorway, holding her stuffty fennec fox by his oversize ears. In keeping with her unvarying system of nomenclature, he is named Mr. Fox.

Maddy's left shoulder is shrugged up as if to block her ear, a premonition of sensory overload. She blinks wide eyed at the scene before her.

Mark and Rebecca are voiceless, caught completely off guard.

The thing-man lowers himself to one knee, making himself small, unthreatening. "How nice to meet you, young lady. Is that Mr. Fox?"

Maddy hugs the fox tight to her chest and rocks back and forth.

"Did you know that the ears of a fennec fox are the largest relative to body size of anyone in the dog family?"

Maddy's face explodes in a smile. "Six inches!" she says. "They grow up to six inches."

"Do you know what they are used for?"

"Radiators!" Maddy says. "Cuz it's hot in the desert, so they have to regulate their body temperature."

She pronounces *regulate* like *reg-goo-late*, and Rebecca feels a surge of unadulterated love for this pure, pure child. And the first premonition of appreciation for whatever this thing is in their nursery.

"I've been wondering," the thing-man says, "are fennec foxes diurnal? Or nocturnal?"

"Nocturnal," Maddy says, a touch shyly.

"Ah. That makes sense. Thank you."

"Welcome."

Mark and Rebecca have been watching the exchange like idiot spectators at a tennis match.

"May I call you Maddy?" the thing-man asks. "Or do you prefer Madeleine?"

"Maddy."

"Thank you, Maddy. What would you like to call me?"

Maddy cocks her head. Her shoulder has lowered, and her arms have loosened, Mr. Fox swaying from her fist. She studies the thing-man, her brow furrowed adorably.

Then she says, "Mr. Man."

Mr. Man nods. "I like that," he says. "What do you say we all get back to bed. We have a big day tomorrow."

"What are you gonna do?"

"I have some cleaning to do in here." Mr. Man nods to the goo-filled prism. And then, to Rebecca: "Would I find more towels in the linen closet?"

Rebecca somehow finds her voice. "Laundry room. Cupboard above the dryer."

"I will do that. And I will see you all in the morning."

"Mr. Fox is awake at night too," Maddy says. "Want him to keep you company?"

"That is so kind, Maddy." Mr. Man presses one hand to his heart. Or, Rebecca supposes, to the place where a heart would be. "I'd be honored."

Maddy trudges over and offers up Mr. Fox.

Is that a wink Mr. Man makes at Maddy with one of his smooth eyes?

Maddy gazes up at him. She looks so small. "Sydney says stuffties are for babies," she confides.

Mr. Man regards Mr. Fox with tenderness. Then he gives Mr. Fox a hug. "It seems like Sydney does not understand stuffties."

"That's right!" Maddy says. "She doesn't. She doesn't get stuffties at all."

Mr. Man makes one of Mr. Fox's hands wave goodnight to Maddy.

"G'night," Maddy tells Mr. Fox and Mr. Man.

"Thank you for having me here," Mr. Man tells them all.

Mark clears his throat. "Sure," he says.

They stand a moment longer and then withdraw awkwardly.

Chapter 11

Rebecca and Mark are curled on their sides in bed, facing each other, noses almost touching, speaking in whispers.

"What did you expect?" Mark asks.

"I don't know. Like an interface. A computer interface that interacts with our smart devices."

"With tentacle arms?"

She gives him a playful smack on the arm. "No. Like digitally or whatever." She leans in, pokes the tip of her nose against his. "How 'bout you?"

"A robot, maybe. Like those blank-faced ones from Japan. A robot butler."

Rebecca sticks out her tongue. "I just thought of something gross."

"What?"

"Remember how Alexa said it's designed for our gratification?"

Mark's features screw themselves up. "Do you think she *has sex* with it?"

"At least it'll keep her off you at the next Christmas party."

They laugh quietly.

Mark asks, "What do you think of it?"

"Him," Rebecca says.

"Gendering him already?"

"He *is* named Mr. Man."

"We should've named him Jeeves."

Rebecca says, "Smithers."

"Alfred."

"Alfred?"

"Batman," Mark clarifies, and Rebecca rolls her eyes. He is such a nerd sometimes.

"What do *you* think of him?" she asks.

"I don't know," Mark says. "It's super weird. Obviously. Let's see. Let's see what happens."

"He seems very polite. And Maddy likes him."

"Yeah," Mark says. "I just didn't count on having another person-like thing in the house."

"If it's too weird, we can always return him."

"We're in charge," Mark quotes archly.

"But it might be nice to have some help around the house. Someone we don't have to worry about. Their feelings and needs, all that. Someone who's just focused on *our* needs."

"It's like the opposite of a baby." The minute the words leave Mark's mouth, his eyes flare. "Oh, I'm sorry, Beccs. I didn't mean it like that."

But the comment doesn't wound as it might have last month, last week, last night. "Maybe this is good," she whispers. "Maybe this is what we need."

Mark smiles, relieved. "Let's get some sleep."

But her heart is thundering, adrenaline still charging through her veins. Her mind fills with concerns, possibilities, opportunities.

She does not get any sleep.

Chapter 12

By the time Rebecca gets dressed, brushes her teeth, and steps into the hall the next morning, the washing machine is whirring and she can smell toast from the kitchen. Maddy is already seated, dressed for school, and her lunch box is on the counter, packed and ready to go. Sitting in the chair beside her, atop a stack of cookbooks, is Mr. Fox, who has a cloth napkin tied around his neck.

Mark is sitting also, hands curled around a cup of coffee, watching on high alert.

In the adjacent family room, the wall-mounted TV is on mute, tuned to CNBC, a perennial stock ticker running across the bottom of the screen. Odd because Mark rarely turns the TV on in the morning.

Rebecca follows Mark's gaze to the strange entity in their kitchen. His movements are smooth, efficient, preterhuman.

His forearms are perfectly even, toes and fingers slightly too proportional.

Mr. Man slides a piece of buttered toast onto Maddy's plate. "A rat he found in the garden," he says, answering a question Rebecca did not hear.

"Any insects?" Maddy asks.

"He could not find any insects last night. But he ate some eggs."

"Mr. Fox, are you full from your rat and eggs? Or do you need 'nother bite?" Maddy brings her empty cereal spoon to Mr. Fox's snout, makes a slurping sound, her best attempt at ventriloquism.

Rebecca leans over, gives Mark a kiss on the cheek. "Good morning."

Mark's eyes do not leave Mr. Man, who is now loading the dishwasher.

"Would you like breakfast, Rebecca?" Mr. Man asks.

"No, thanks."

"Or should I call you Beccs?"

Mark says, a touch sharply, "Rebecca is fine."

Mr. Man nods. "Mark, would you like a top-off of your coffee?"

"I'm good," Mark says. Then to Rebecca: "Why don't I take Maddy to school? You can stay and . . . figure all this out?"

"Yay! Daddy Carpool!"

When Mark drives Maddy, he swerves playfully and they sing along to the Disney Channel on Sirius with fake opera voices. He is so much fun.

Rebecca says, "Sure."

Mark stands up, puts his hands on her shoulders, looks down into her eyes, his most tender gaze. "You okay?" he asks quietly. "You nervous about any of this?"

"Of course I'm nervous," Rebecca says. But then she adds, "I got it," and is surprised to know that she means it.

Mark studies her a moment longer. "Okay. I'll keep my phone on, even in meetings. Anything comes up. *Anything*."

Rebecca nods.

Maddy slingshots herself out of her chair, runs to the door to the garage, hopping up and down. "Daddy Carpool! Let's go, let's go!"

"Coming, child!" Mark says in his funny, gruff voice.

"Bye, Mr. Man!" Maddy gives an exuberant wave.

Mr. Man straightens up from the dishwasher, returns the wave. "Have a great day at school, Maddy. Mr. Fox and I will hold down the encampment."

"Fort." Maddy giggles. "Hold down the *fort*."

She is beaming as she heads into the garage. Rebecca cannot remember the last time she has seen Maddy head to school cheerfully. She is normally riddled with anxiety about what Sydney and the Mean Girls have in store.

Rebecca braces herself and then turns on her phone. *Ding ding ding*—texts and notifications pour in. The useless blow-and-go gardener wants a raise. She needs to bring allergy-free snacks for the upcoming student showcase night. Their accountant needs her and Mark to Docusign some kind of a release for last year's taxes.

She can already feel her chest tightening in the face of the demands of the day.

When she looks up, Mr. Man is studying her from across the kitchen.

She hoists her phone. "So much happening."

Mr. Man closes his eyes. His lids flicker, as if from REM. His eyes open again. "I see," he says.

And she understands that he means it literally, that he is wired into their network, into her. And yet she is not creeped out. She feels understood, somehow. Seen.

She tries on a request: "I'll have a cup of coffee. I'm exhausted."

"Why don't you go back to sleep?"

She laughs. "I can't possibly, not with what's lining up for—" She catches herself.

"Can you handle . . . ?" She isn't sure what she is asking, how to finish.

"I will clean the kitchen, run the dishwasher. I can put away the dishes."

"How do you know where they go?"

"I know your routine in the kitchen." Mr. Man nods at the flat-screen in the family room. "Built-in camera in the smart TV."

As Rebecca looks, the trading symbol for Mark's company coasts across the ticker. She can't make out the number, but the red arrow pointing down is clear as day, and it hits her why Mark wanted to keep an eye on the TV this morning.

Bao-Bao rattles in his cage.

"The rest of the chores can be completed in order on the basis of your value hierarchy," Mr. Man says. "I will feed the rabbit and clean the cage. Sort and fold the laundry. The backyard furniture needs cleaning from bird droppings. And I can pick up Maddy's meds at Walgreens. I know the route through your vehicle's GPS."

"You can *drive*?"

"My special testing permit is on file at the DMV, as well as a license to operate on public roads. Same as a self-driving Tesla or autopiloted Waymo. But safer."

"Can you go out in public?"

"If I wear a hat and sunglasses, I can pass for normal. Especially in a vehicle or at night."

"You sure you can . . . do all this?"

Mr. Man's eyes close, and the eyelids flicker once more. "I will have these tasks completed by 11:37 a.m."

Rebecca is finding this hard to believe. No—worse than that. She is finding it hard to let go of her urge to be in charge of the very chores that plague her. What is it? A need for control? A need to be a martyr?

She closes her eyes just like Mr. Man, tries to access a different part of herself. Then she says, "Do you need something to eat? I mean, how does this work?"

"I do not have a digestive system. Or excretory. My only operational requirement is that I recharge in my bed at intervals. I do not require anything from you. I am here only to help. You are in charge."

She tries to leave again, but her feet won't budge. "Can I . . . Can I touch you?"

"Of course."

She approaches cautiously. Wonder overpowers fear.

She reaches out her finger. It trembles slightly.

He mirrors her movement. Their fingertips touch, an *ET*–Sistine Chapel moment.

Feels just like human skin.

A gasp escapes her.

Mr. Man lowers his arm. "Get some rest, Rebecca. I can take it from here."

She tears herself away, pads down the hall.

Once she's back between the sheets, exhaustion rushes her. She is surprised to find that she welcomes it.

Chapter 13

Maddy hates recess. She never knows where to go. The Popular Boys are on the monkey bars. Sydney and the Mean Girls are at their picnic table over by the slide, comparing pictures on their phones. Maddy senses their presence at all times like heat—when they have entered the cafeteria, the classroom, when they are behind her at kiss-and-ride drop-off.

Clutching her lunch box, she debates hiding in the library and eating behind the science-and-technology bookcase, but there is no food or beverages in the library and she got caught once already and she doesn't like breaking rules and getting in trouble.

She decides to go to the science room to eat with Mrs. Gower, but it is too late. They have spotted her.

"Hey, Maddy! Over here." Sydney is standing on the picnic table bench now, waving her over with a big smile, and Maddy thinks maybe, just maybe, this one time Sydney will be kind.

My voice matters, she reminds herself.

Eyes lowered, she clutches the insulated lunch box before her with both hands. It knocks against her knees as she walks over. She wishes Mommy was here to make her Nervous Tummy Tea. Even though she is wearing her short dress, she is sweating.

"Look, guys," Sydney says in her Sydney voice, "it's Ms. Maddy."

Maddy's stomach is tight and her throat is tight and she worries she might cry. She tells herself, *I tried my best today.*

"Nice lunch box," Girl Dylan says. "Is that a dino on it?"

Still staring at the asphalt, Maddy nods.

"You can look at us, you know," Sydney says. "You *do* know how to make eye contact?"

Maddy forces herself to lift her gaze. Everything is so bright all of a sudden, so bright it hurts her eyes. The girls' cell phone screens flash, and the metal slide is glinting in the hot afternoon sun.

"Dylly asked you a question," Sydney says. "Is that a dino on your big-girl lunch box?"

Maddy nods again, her chin quivering. They have been hard at work on their "These Are a Few of My Favorite Things" displays for student showcase night, and Maddy's crayon drawings feature dinosaurs prominently.

"What kind of dino?" Sydney says. "A . . . *Maddysaurus*?"

Maddy hates that they overheard Mommy call her that.

She answers quietly: "Stegosaurus."

Brayed laughter.

"That's so *cool*," McKenzie says in a not-nice voice. "Can you tell us something about stegosauruses?"

I am still growing and learning.

"They were as long as a bus," Maddy says quietly. "And they had tiny brains the size of a walnut."

"Kinda like you?" Sydney says, and they all laugh.

"I have what it takes." Maddy is horrified to hear that she has spoken her last affirmation out loud.

"Do you? Do you *really*, Maddy?"

Tears spill, hot on her cheeks. She looks around, but the yard monitor is over by the recycle bin, scolding Boy Dylan, who is almost as bad as Girl Dylan.

Her hands are starting to shake, and she doesn't want to stim, not here in front of everyone, but the sensations are overpowering, the girls' laughter and the tightness in her stomach and the hot, hot sun. She wishes Mr. Fox were here, and she remembers that even though fennec foxes are small, they can jump as high as a meter, and she feels a sudden fierce pride to be as mighty as a fennec fox.

"Yes," she says fiercely, hearing her lisp on the *s.*

Sydney eases off the bench and walks over to her. Sydney is taller, so Maddy is looking at her necklace, a pendant with *Choose Kindness* written in cursive.

"If you have what it takes . . ." Sydney stoops down to find Maddy's eyes with hers. It feels like getting stabbed in the brain. "Then why don't you *show* us?"

Maddy wipes at her cheeks roughly, sets her jaw. "How?"

Chapter 14

Sleeping until 11:00 a.m.!

For the first time Rebecca can remember, she feels well rested. She awakens to the susurration of a gentle breeze moving through the Y-shaped pine outside. Bobbing branches and needle patterns wash the closed window shade.

She takes a long, hot shower, taking extra time with the handheld showerhead. She washes her hair, and then blow-dries it for the first time in over a year. She moisturizes her face, lotions her body, clips her nails. When she steps into the hall, the house smells of coffee.

Mr. Man is finishing cleaning out Bao-Bao's cage. The dishes are put away, the counters spotless, and Maddy's prescription refill bottle rests on Rebecca's tiny work desk in the kitchen. Fresh coffee burbles in the pot.

Mr. Man rises, bag of trash in hand. "I purchased some Kenyan beans for you. Your Facebook post from 368 days ago said they were your favorite. I hope they are still. Would you like me to pour you a cup?"

Overcome with gratitude, she nods.

He serves her coffee and then steps outside to dispose of the trash bag.

She sits at the table. It is already set for dinner. She almost cannot believe it.

What is it she plans to do with her one wild and precious day? She cannot remember the last time she went to a movie, read a magazine, a novel. It's astounding and shameful how busy she always is, given how many resources she has around her, an affluent mother in Brentwood with a single child and no need to hunt and gather, to start fires or raise barn frames, to fight off saber-toothed tigers or roving bands of pirates. The more technology improves, the worse she seems to feel. But maybe this is the turning point.

She closes her eyes, breathes in the fresh-ground Kenyan blend. A tiny sip proves it is as delicious as she remembers from 368 days ago.

Her exhale keeps going, as if she is letting go of months of pressure, which perhaps she is. She takes another sip.

Her phone rings.

Caller ID shows it is Maddy's emergency cell.

When she taps to answer, Maddy is screaming uncontrollably.

Chapter 15

As Rebecca screeches into a handicap space at the school and flies from the minivan, she can hear Maddy's cries all the way over in the nurse's office. She sprints through the corridors, passing open classroom doors, students' heads swiveling to watch her blaze by.

Having Mr. Man at the house was a godsend—he registered her state with a single look and held the door to the garage open for her, keys resting on his gray palm. On the drive over, she called Mark three times, but despite his promise, he did not pick up.

When she bursts into the nurse's office, Maddy's screams intensify; the sight of her mother has made it safe for her to access even greater anguish. Maddy lies on the padded exam table, her short dress pulled up. A bright-red burn mars her left hip, like a raspberry from sliding across gravel. It is already starting to bubble at the edges. There are ice packs wrapped in paper towels and water in a bucket and gauze pads. The principal is there, as well as the yard monitor.

Maddy is hysterical, rocking violently, chewing the collar of her dress, flapping her hands. Rebecca steps past the agitated nurse, and Maddy clutches at her. Rebecca presses Maddy's ear to her chest and breathes deep and slow, mirroring the respiration Maddy needs to slow herself down.

It is a process.

Maddy migrates from screaming to inconsolable sobbing. "Daddy! I want Daddy!"

Rebecca rocks her, dialing and dialing again. All the while her phone hasn't stopped dinging—dentist confirmation for next week, her long-suffering mother, the supermom kiss-and-ride scheduler, and it looks like she missed the fucking solar repair guy again.

Amid all this, she manages to piece together what happened from the nurse, the yard monitor, and the principal. Evidently Sydney and her crew bullied Maddy into going down the slide like a big girl, knowing the metal was hot enough to burn.

Rebecca is livid.

She breathes steadily, still cupping Maddy's cheek against her chest, one hand flat against Maddy's other ear to diminish audio stimulation. Maddy murmurs, "Daddy, want Daddy," over and over again, Rebecca's heart disintegrating with each wail.

Principal de La Rosa is equal parts empathetic and apprehensive. "The metal equipment is supposed to be off limits on days with temperatures over ninety degrees," she says, shooting a look of admonishment at the yard monitor. "We've had it agenda-ed for two quarters to swap the slide out for plastic, but you know how funding is right now with LA Unified. We're making do until Parent Givefest next month. We really can't afford any . . . additional expenses."

Maddy is still snuffling against Rebecca's chest.

"Don't worry, Veronica," Rebecca says. "We're not gonna sue you."

Principal de La Rosa visibly exhales.

"But," Rebecca continues, through clenched teeth, "I want a meeting with Sydney's parents."

Chapter 16

Exiting the conference room, Mark hurries back to his office. A fast-moving competitor has swanned into their area code of the market, picking off client accounts, so projections are down even further, stock price is bleeding, and he is behind schedule for the product-upgrade launch. His team is integrating AI chatbots into the customer-service modules, but they'd run into a rat's nest of problems dealing with data integration, about 20 percent of which are of his team's making. The other 80 percent rests squarely on the shoulders of Derek, whose micro-mismanagement is typical of a business guy overseeing tech.

Derek has become increasingly ill tempered and tyrannical, his frustrations finding the best target in Mark, and Mark has had little choice but to keep his head down, work harder, and take it.

He has been managing the corporate turbulence as best he can, trying not to dump additional stress on Rebecca, given everything she and her body have been through in the past year, but he fears he is bottling up more than he can handle. His acid reflux is up again, his patience down, nerves worn thin.

He closes his office door, thumps his shoulders against it, tilts his head to the ceiling, and exhales. When he fishes his muted phone from his pocket, he sees seven missed calls from his wife.

Panic flares.

Getting dressed down in front of his team had taken enough of his focus that he'd forgotten about Mr. Man.

He dials.

Rebecca picks up on a half ring.

"Are you okay?" Mark says. "Did he do something?"

"What? No. I'm at school."

Rebecca rattles off enough details for him to understand what happened. He sinks into his Aeron, which heaves gently back, catching his weight. Rubbing his forehead, he listens and listens some more.

Across his computer monitor is the schedule for the launch, pushed back for the third time in as many weeks after Derek threw out the product road map and changed direction yet again.

Mark's unread email count is bolded at 289. A pall of despondency descends on him. What is he doing with this job, his life? Why is he here in this sterile office instead of with his family? Studying computer engineering and dating Beccs, he'd had expansive hopes for himself. They'd planned on having a passel of kids, bunk beds in each room, crowded Christmas card photos. The internet boom had been all about prosperity and flourishing, making the world a better place.

And yet, somehow he's found himself tasked with replacing human workers with AI, putting people out of jobs. The free market would correct that with its brutal expediency, as it always did. Workers would be retrained to fix AI until AI could be trained to fix AI, then humans would have to be trained to do . . . what? He thinks of the thing-man in his house right now, filling some void he hadn't realized he and Rebecca needed filled.

He stares at the framed photo on his desk, him and Rebecca at the beach, Maddy on his shoulders smeared with zinc sunscreen and wearing only a swim diaper. She was two years old, a few months before the diagnosis. They are all laughing, a happy family of three. He wishes he was there in the photo on that beach before diagnoses and miscarriages, when the tracks had still led to a future that made sense.

When Rebecca pauses to take a breath, he says, "How is she?"

"Exhausted," Beccs says. "Beyond exhausted. She's sleeping now. I'm gonna let her rest, then take her home."

"Good," he says. "Good."

"When can you get here?"

Mark catches himself rubbing his forehead some more. "I don't know."

"She was crying for you, Mark." Her voice wobbles and then cracks. "She wouldn't stop crying for you. You need to get here. You need to make her smile."

"Okay," Mark says. "Okay. Gimme a sec. Call right back."

With apprehension mounting, he exits his office, strolls across the floor past rows of cubicles, and knuckle-taps the open door to Derek's office.

Behind his desk, Derek looks up at Mark and resumes typing on his computer. No acknowledgment, no gesture.

Mark walks in and stands awkwardly before the desk. The view is vast, overlooking a swath of the Westside and the rise of the Santa Monicas, the Hollywood sign visible in the distance.

Two minutes pass.

Five.

Centered on the large square coffee table is a bold red-and-blue book called *The 48 Laws of Power*. A brass-framed photograph of Alexa in a plunging-neckline dress rests on Derek's desk, pointedly aimed outward. It's an 8 × 10, the kind actresses use for headshots. Alexa's lips are pursed, her index finger resting along her clavicle. The bookcase behind Derek's desk displays not books but miniature Porsche model cars. The decor suits a sophomore in college.

Mark clears his throat.

Derek glares up at him. *"What?"*

"I have to go," he says. "I'm sorry. Maddy's been injured."

"Injured injured? Like she broke a leg?"

"She got burned. On a slide."

"Burned on a slide," Derek says, tapping his Montblanc against the leather blotter. "Third degree? Fourth?"

Mark feels the hinges of his jaw tighten, tells himself to loosen his expression. "I don't think that bad. But she's sensitive."

"Yes," Derek said. "Know who else is sensitive?"

He waits, but Mark does not give him the satisfaction of inquiring.

"Me. I'm sensitive. Know *why* I'm sensitive, Mark? Because one of my fucking chief product officers is three weeks behind schedule—wait, no, make that *four* weeks behind schedule, and my stock price is in the shitter. Know how much money I've lost in the past two months, Mark?"

Mark, too, has lost 60 percent of his unrealized holdings, though he'd started with a substantially lesser sum.

"You need to prioritize work right now, Mark, like the rest of us."

"I've been working eleven-hour days, Derek. For weeks straight now."

"When Elon was spinning up Tesla, he slept in a conference room in the factory." Derek exhales, rubs his temples in circles. "We're assessing promotions next quarter. I'll give you a sneak peek now: You're not getting one. If you want to hold steady, have a second shot at delivering what is in your purview to deliver, you won't run out of here midday every time your kid gets a scrape or a bee sting."

Heat boils up in Mark, scours his throat. He tastes the bile at the back of his mouth, acid and rage. He does not trust himself to speak.

"I gave you the plus-one invite from N0RM LLC. You have another man at home to handle anything and everything. So how 'bout you let him handle it? And you handle your responsibilities here."

He goes back to his laptop.

Mark stands there for ten seconds. Twenty.

Derek does not look up.

Mark exits.

Walks on numb legs back to his office. Closes the door. Sits down at his desk. He fills with fury and shame. Shame is worse.

He makes a fist to slam onto his desk but stops just shy and then presses the pinkie edge to the wood. A few deep breaths.

He calls Rebecca back.

"Hey, Beccs. I can't make it there. I'm sorry. Derek is being a total—"

"What do you mean you can't make it? She was a mess, Mark. She was asking for you and only you. She needs her dad right now."

"I can't leave, Rebecca."

"I get you're balancing a lot with the upgrade and Dickhead Derek, but this was a bad one. Maddy needs you right now."

"My *job* is on the line. This is the real world, not—" He catches himself, chest heaving.

"Not *what?*"

"Nothing. I'm just saying, someone has to pay for all this. Especially after this quarter-of-a-million-dollar boondoggle."

"That was *my* choice?"

His teeth are clenched. "I'm not saying that."

"And it's not a boondoggle, it's an—"

"*Investment*. Right."

A long pause. He can hear her breathing.

"Why don't you just stand up to Derek?"

"And what?" he says. "Get fired?"

"No. Set boundaries."

His temper ignites before he can squash it. "Right. I'll take lessons on that from you."

He squeezes his eyes shut.

When Rebecca's voice comes after the excruciating pause, it is very, very quiet. "We don't do that. We aren't sarcastic with each other."

He knows he should apologize, that he eventually will apologize, but he cannot muster the fortitude to do so now. Not after getting emasculated in Derek's office.

He rubs his eyes hard, colors kaleidoscoping behind the lids. "How is she now?"

"Still sleeping. I'm gonna take her home."

"Can I . . ." His voice shakes, but he steadies it. "Can I hear her? Breathing?"

The word comes pert and hard: "Sure."

A rustling noise, and then he hears his daughter's little whistling breaths, shallow as a newborn's.

He listens.

Covers his mouth.

And tries not to cry.

Chapter 17

Driving home, Rebecca marvels at how Maddy can slumber after a fit. She knocks out like a baby. If Rebecca were to reach into the back seat and lift her eyelids, they would snap right back shut.

Despite the air-conditioning on high, Rebecca is sweating profusely. Her hormones still roar about, especially when she gets emotional, which is always.

She is furious with Mark.

She loves Mark.

But she is furious with him.

As she coasts up their street, she spots Jackson standing on his roof with a broom, sweeping briskly, angrily. Her body temperature spikes precipitously. He pauses to glare at her as she coasts past and banks into her driveway. Even once he is wiped from view, his angry, frozen form remains, a dark spot floating at the edge of her peripheral vision.

She shifts into park, her other hand already fumbling at the garage-door opener, rushing to close herself off from the outside world.

Hustling, she eases Maddy from her car seat, careful not to brush against the gauze bandaging. Maddy lolls in her arms, head thrown back, throat exposed.

Rebecca's back aches. Maddy is too old to be carried, and yet she must be carried.

As she fumbles at the door to the kitchen, it suddenly opens and there is Mr. Man, light from the window above the sink streaming over his shoulders.

Effortlessly, he lifts Maddy from her arms. A folder on the kitchen counter bears the logo of the solar repair company. Another small blessing: Mr. Man must have overseen the appointment while Rebecca was at the nurse's, one thing to cross off the ever-replenishing checklist.

As they move down the hall, they stay hushed, despite the impossibility of waking Maddy in this state. Mr. Man follows Rebecca's direction, lowering Maddy into bed.

Rebecca taps the sound soother on, hoping the white noise rush will allow Maddy to slumber.

They file mutely back into the kitchen, and Rebecca plops down heavily at the nicely set table, Mr. Man sitting across from her. She lowers her face into her hands.

Mr. Man's flat yet pleasing voice breaks the sound of her heavy breathing: "Would you like me to get you anything?"

If she speaks, she will break down, so she just shakes her head.

The doorbell rings.

She starts at the sound. The chime, like a violation.

Mr. Man cocks his head inquisitively.

She shakes her head.

It rings again.

Then there comes an angry pounding at the door.

"Open up, Rebecca! I know you're in there! I just *saw* you get home!"

The pounding intensifies, turns menacing, the violence of fist slamming wood. She prays the noise won't rouse Maddy.

"Get out here and look at what I just swept off my fucking roof!"

Mr. Man is still looking at Rebecca solicitously.

She says, "Will you just . . . sit here with me?"

More hammering.

Rebecca's blouse, smeared with sweat and Maddy's tears, clings to her. She closes her eyes, covers her ears.

Please stop, she thinks. *Please just stop.*

Finally the pounding ceases.

After a few seconds of silence, she lowers her hands from her ears.

Mr. Man reaches across the table, rests a cool, comforting hand on her forearm. "It's okay," he says, "Beccs."

Chapter 18

As Rebecca re-dresses Maddy's wound, Mr. Man finishes the pasta she started and makes a salad as directed. The house is spotless, every chore complete before Rebecca can think of it. The relief she feels upon entering the kitchen borders on ecstatic.

Sitting with them, Mr. Man is motionless, but his presence doesn't feel eerie, just peaceful. He is wearing one of Mark's T-shirts and the same pair of jeans, and he looks almost normal.

Rebecca has been nursing her resentment at Mark for the past hour, but when his text arrives, she hastens to read it.

Sorry I was an asshole. I love you.

In an instant, everything is forgiven.
Sorry I was a bitch, she types back. I love you, too.

She sends a black-and-white romantic hand-holding GIF. He *hearts* it.

Things are really rough with Derek. I need to be here late.

She sends a naggy-wife-shaking-a-rolling-pin GIF and types: Why don't you just stand up to him?
He *ha-ha*s it.
Sends back a giant-bearded-biker-guy-on-a-Harley GIF, replies: Cuz SOMEONE'S gotz ta pay for everything up in here!
Her fist is against her mouth, muffling her laughter.
She is about to put her phone away when another text arrives, this one from Principal de La Rosa: Evidently Don Evans is out of town but Sheila has agreed to meet you at her house tomorrow at five p.m. I hope this works for you. Looking forward to getting on the same page and putting this all behind us!
It takes a moment for Rebecca to put together that the principal is referring to Sydney's parents.
"No phones at the table, Mommy," Maddy says.
"You're right. Sorry, kiddo."
She *thumbs-up*s the text, puts her phone away.
Rebecca will keep her daughter home from school tomorrow, unwilling to have her face her bully until Rebecca has said her piece to the bully's mother.

Maddy hasn't eaten much, just shoved the pasta around in its division on her sectioned plate that keeps different foods from touching one another. In his cage, Bao-Bao clamors to be fed.

"Would you like to start her nigh-night routine?" Mr. Man says. "I can finish cleaning up in here."

Rebecca pauses on her way out to make eye contact. "Thank you."

Mr. Man gives a faint nod.

The bath takes longer than ever. Keeping the drain open, Rebecca runs lukewarm water and carefully sponges around the red patch of flesh, Maddy's eyes screwed up tight, her body rigid. Gingerly applied soap, no-tears shampoo, careful pat-pat-pat to dry, lotion but not on the burn, brush teeth, pee, princess nightgown. As they head to the kitchen to give Bao-Bao goodnight kisses, Mr. Man comes in from the backyard with a stubby leaf in his hand.

He lowers himself to one knee, shows Maddy the glistening seam where it has been snapped off. "Do you know what this is, Maddy?"

Maddy chews her bottom lip, examines the offering. "Aloe vera."

"Do you know what it is used for?"

She nods. "But what if it hurts?"

"Perhaps you could hold it and apply it yourself?" he says.

She takes the leaf and examines it a moment, still working at her lip. "Didja know that orangutans sometimes use plants to heal owies?"

"I did indeed," Mr. Man says. "They are so brave."

Maddy draws in a breath. Then she hikes up her Belle-from-*Beauty-and-the-Beast* nightgown and holds the fleshy leaf hovering above the burn. Scrunching her eyes shut, she swipes it across the puffy skin, leaving a film of gel.

She opens her eyes again, draws in a shaky breath, and hands the leaf back.

A smile. "I did it."

"You sure did," Mr. Man says.

Back to Maddy's bedroom for stuffties *sleep tight* hugs. Then fluff pillows, tuck blankets to the chin, *Horton Hears a Who!* and *Good Night, Gorilla*. During *Goodnight Moon*, Maddy finds the mouse on each page, sounding out the words as Rebecca reads. Next it's time for sleep-inducing nose pets and activating Pillow Pet's projected stars on the ceiling. After they count the stars, it's time to make wishes.

"I wish kids at school liked me," Maddy says, without a trace of self-pity.

Protective fury flashes, and then Rebecca careens into utter heartbreak. It envelopes her like quicksand, promising to pull her down, her and everything else around her.

"They *do* like you, Maddysaurus."

"Don't lie to me," Maddy says, with a spike of anger. "And don't *call* me that. Not ever again."

Rebecca recoils internally, a sea anemone curling into itself. She knows this isn't about the nickname, that this is a venting of hurt, but even so, Maddy's tone wounds her.

Before she can regain her composure, Maddy turns away, tucking in Mr. Fox. Then she settles back on the pillow and begins her nighttime affirmations: "My voice matters."

Biting back tears in the semidarkness, Rebecca strokes her daughter's silky hair.

"I tried my best today." Maddy's blue eyes are wide and thoughtful. "I did, Mommy. I really did."

Rebecca makes sure to keep her voice even: "I know."

Maddy tugs at Mr. Fox's ears. "I am still growing and learning."

Rebecca nods encouragingly.

And then, in the tiniest whisper: "I have what it takes." Maddy curls her fingers around Rebecca's thumb. "Mommy?"

"Yes, Maddysaur—" She catches herself. "Yes, sweetheart?"

"What if I *don't*?"

Rebecca can barely manage words. "You *do* have what it takes." Is it true? A half lie? A wish? "Of course you do."

She kisses Maddy on the forehead and slips from the room.

Chapter 19

It is the first time Rebecca has left Maddy with Mr. Man. With Mark at work and the meeting with Sydney's mother at 5:00 p.m., she has little choice. Maddy seems delighted to be with Mr. Man, and Rebecca will keep her phone on, and it will just be a brief visit.

The residence on North Tigertail Road is less house than estate. The sight of numerous luxury SUVs parked in the roundabout driveway gives Rebecca pause.

The front doors are enormous, two stories high, wrought-iron and glass, looking into a foyer the size of Rebecca and Mark's backyard. A staircase sweeps up to floors unseen. On the landing wall, an enormous Lichtenstein beams red and yellow Ben Day dots. A beady black eye of a lens peers out from the modern doorbell, and yet the chime sounds throaty, like a medieval organ.

Footsteps patter.

An attractive woman appears, a pencil skirt constraining gym-slim hips, a glamorous cashmere cape swept around her sequin camisole, rakishly barefoot. Sydney's mom—Sheila—waves; her other arm, bent angularly, terminates in a sleek bowl of white wine. Given the expanse, it takes some time for her to reach the door, and they hold eye contact through the glass. Rebecca shifts awkwardly on the porch, wishing she'd changed out of her mom jeans.

"You must be Maddy's mommy," Sheila says, her smile pronounced between sexy, augmented lips. Sheila offers an icy hug, contorting at the waist, head thrown wide, face turned away, a skeletal pat of Rebecca's back. Her powerful perfume, lavender and citrus, calls to mind Derek's wife, Alexa.

Mean Girls, Rebecca thinks, as she follows Sheila back.

A massive bearskin hugs the marble before a hearth the size of a Cybertruck. "Don't worry," Sheila says breezily, "not real."

They pass staff everywhere, chefs moving briskly in the kitchen, maids scurrying past, cleaning crews dusting and bustling. A decorator-type resets basketballs in a tank of water, a Jeff Koons–like installation or, more likely, an actual Jeff Koons. A butler halts his progress to stand at attention against a wall as they pass. Rebecca's midwestern upbringing flares, and she gives him a smile. He returns a nearly imperceptible nod.

Sheila leads Rebecca down a corridor wide enough to accommodate a subway train. "The girls and I are just down here," she says, and Rebecca feels her stomach constrict at the notion of an ambush.

Sure enough, there the girls are, spread around divans and couches, each more expensively curated than the next. Pearls glitter; jewels match ear to wrist; hairdos present with professional severity. The room is like a salon from the Roaring Twenties designed by someone obsessed with taupe. Introductions are made, Rebecca failing to keep up with the names.

"Glass of Vermentino?" Sheila asks.

Rebecca has never heard the word and does not want a drink. "No, thank you."

One of the women, a wide-mouthed brunette says, "This is *sooo* much better than the Viognier."

Rebecca scratches her shoulder, realizes she is doing it, stops. "I'm sorry," she says, cursing herself for apologizing even as she's doing it. "I didn't realize I was interrupting a social gathering."

"Oh, this isn't social," Sheila says.

"Well, everything *we* do is a *bit* social," says the redhead, running manicured nails through a faux-fur throw on the divan.

"Given your concerns," Sheila continues, "I thought I'd get all the girls together from, you know, our daughters' group."

Maddy does not have a group. And if she did, it certainly wouldn't be composed of the offspring of these harpies.

"I know Maddy has been uncomfortable—"

"No," Rebecca says, "she's been bullied."

"That's *one* version of events," says another woman, East Asian, severe makeup, world-class legs crossed high at the thigh beneath a micro-mini Rebecca might have been able to fit into when she was twelve. "But everyone has their own."

"*Especially* girls," the redhead chimes in. "I mean, half the stories we get are 'She said, she said, she said.'"

"Maddy sustained a bad burn," Rebecca says, somehow defending herself, her injured child. She admonishes herself mentally for resorting to the dramatically medical *sustained*.

"We understand that, sweetie, and we feel *terrible* about it," the brunette says, "but everything that happens doesn't have to be someone's *fault*. I mean, they're children. And children play."

"Maddy was bullied into getting on that slide."

"Bullied," the redhead laughs, with a roll of her head.

"Yes," Rebecca says. "Bullied."

Sheila lays a too-thin hand on Rebecca's arm. "I mean, can we really believe her story, what with her sensitivities and filters and . . . limitations and whatnot?"

Unprepared for a direct attack on her daughter, Rebecca is stunned into speechlessness.

"We can't slow down a whole village to accommodate one child," another woman says, somewhere behind Rebecca, by the leather-padded bar.

Sheila pivots in front of Rebecca, an assault of high-end perfume and aggressively sympathetic eyes: "What we're saying is, Maddy really seems to be struggling with her mental health."

"She's not struggling," Rebecca says through clenched teeth, though of course Maddy is. "She just needs to not be bullied."

"Look, Rebecca, we're here to talk mothers-to-mother," Sheila says. "And we wanted to present the possibility that maybe another place could meet Maddy's needs better."

Rebecca realizes then that the situation is hopeless, that she is outmatched and outgunned, that she lost before she even arrived here in this adult playpen of a room. She stares at the panorama of made-up eyes, those oft-injected doll faces not quite capable of arranging themselves into expressions of human warmth. Smugness shines through the thin veneer of feigned empathy, the secret triumph of the ascendant mother.

They are more robotic than Mr. Man.

Rebecca's face is hot, her throat constricting. But she will not give them the satisfaction of seeing her lose her composure. She turns crisply and walks out.

Behind her, voices quickly resume, a hushed murmur.

Oh my God, do you think she's okay?

Should one of us go after her?

Poor thing. Can you even imagine?

Like daughter, like mother.

Rebecca holds a crisp pace. Visible through doorways and windows, house employees bustle like animated characters on a Disney ride, making beds, folding cloth napkins, dipping through the black sheet of an infinity pool to test the pH level.

Finally Rebecca enters the massive foyer, but with every step she takes, the front doors seem to recede. The Lichtenstein notes her progress, unimpressed.

She's just reached the door when she hears, "Ms. Rebecca?"

Her kiss-and-ride name.

She turns.

Sydney stands at the lip of another preposterously wide hallway, dwarfed by the architectural scale. Behind her, fifteen feet down the hall, stands a squat, dour-faced woman, who Rebecca takes to be the watchful nanny.

Wearing a navy blue cardigan sweater against the mausoleum chill, Sydney looks young and lost.

Rebecca registers the slightest softening in her momma-bear heart.

"I didn't think she'd get burned, like, for real," Sydney says, twisting her wrist loosely in her opposite hand.

"Even so," Rebecca says, not unkindly, "it was mean."

Sydney nods and then nods again. "Sorry."

"No more, okay? No more mean."

Sydney lowers her face. "She screamed real loud."

"Yes," Rebecca says. "She did."

Tears dot the marble tile at Sydney's feet. She lets go of the wrist she's been rubbing, and that's when Rebecca sees it, feather-like bruising along her forearm from where it has been grabbed.

"Tell her I'm sorry," Sydney says.

Despite her best efforts, Rebecca feels her anger melt away. "Okay, honey," she says. "I will."

Chapter 20

It is nearly eleven o'clock at night when the doorbell rings.

It is striking how menacing an ordinary sound can be at an unexpected time.

Rebecca fumbles for Mark before remembering that he is still at the office. His mornings start earlier and earlier, his nights ending later. Rebecca can't remember the last time she's seen him in daylight.

Rolling over, she grabs her phone, checks the video doorbell app. No one there, no sign of a car at the curb. A late-night delivery?

Did she dream it?

Out of bed, into her dowdy bathrobe that Mark bought her for the hospital when she was pregnant with Maddy, the one she kept with hopeful anticipation and now cannot bring herself to part with.

After checking the yard from the living room and sidelight windows, she finally musters the courage to open the front door and step onto the porch. Her bare feet stick to the concrete, and she looks down in horror to see

—red-brown spatter on the matte porcelain floor tiles—

something spread across the porch, thick like blood, like matter

—crimson handprint on the side of the bathtub—

and she is already screaming by the time she lifts her feet, high-stepping idiotically in the paste that she sees now is merely sap, sap scraped off Jackson's roof and smeared vengefully across their porch.

"Mommy, what's wrong? What's wrong, Mo—"

And now Maddy has rushed to her side, embracing her hips, and her bare feet, too, are mired in the sap that Jackson caked on their doorstep, and she is screaming, on sensory overload. Rebecca snaps into real time, calming herself, trying to soothe Maddy.

"It's okay, Maddy. It's just sap. Mommy got confused. I just—"

But Maddy is already fully gone, not workable. She's stomping her feet in an agony of hypersensitivity, stimming violently, eyes smashed shut, hands flapping. Rebecca scoops her up to get her off the sticky layer of sap, but Maddy thrashes against her, and she has to tighten her grip, shushing her, rocking her.

"It's okay. We're gonna wash it right off."

A flutter of movement next door pulls her eye, and she spots Jackson in his living room window. His face doesn't look triumphant, not at all. In fact, it wears an uncharacteristic expression of regret. He pulls back, and the curtains fall forward, washing him from view.

Maddy is still howling to wake up the neighborhood.

"Ssh ssh sshhh. Maddy, I got you, baby girl. We're just gonna—"

A hand sets down on Rebecca's shoulder.

She yelps.

Mr. Man stands inside just across the threshold, hidden in shadow. He notes her concern, looks down at the porch and then back up at her. "Would you like me to take care of this?"

She feels an urge to hug him, this strange man with smooth features. "Yes. Thank you."

Still hushing Maddy, she shuffles inside, halting to look at the tar-like footprints she is tracking across the vinyl tiles of their tiny foyer.

Mr. Man holds an arm wide to direct her back toward Maddy's bathroom.

Chapter 21

Maddy can't tolerate the smell of rubbing alcohol so Rebecca scrubs her feet with olive oil. It takes a while, but that's okay because another tantrum would take even longer.

Maddy sits on the edge of the bathtub, slumped sleepily as Rebecca kneels inside, warm olive oil water sloshing around her knees. By the time she is done, Maddy is exhausted enough to go right to bed.

Rebecca tucks her in and eases from the bedroom. She stands a moment in the hall, hand on the doorknob, and exhales a long breath at the ceiling.

She peers up the hall, but there are no sap marks anymore from their feet. The tiles shine pristinely.

Retracing her steps, she marvels at the cleaning job. She passes the nursery's open door, the prism's lid standing open, a grand piano effect.

She expects to find Mr. Man outside on the porch, but he is nowhere in sight.

The porch, too, is spotless, the smell of rubbing alcohol heavy in the air.

That's how he managed to clean everything up so swiftly.

Glaring at Jackson's unlit house, she calls Mark at the office.

"Hi, Beccs, just on a Zoom with Taiwan, crunching some numbers. I'll be outta here in a few. Can we talk when I get home?"

"Yes," she says. "Sure."

He clicks off, neglecting to say goodbye.

She withdraws into the house, throws the dead bolt, checks the kitchen. No sign of Mr. Man there, either, but Bao-Bao thumps in his cage, wanting love. Rebecca takes him out and cuddles him, rubbing her face in the velvet-soft fur of his neck. She looks out into the backyard, but it, too, is empty.

She puts Bao-Bao away and pads quietly down the hall.

As she passes the nursery, a dark form in the corner startles her. It takes a moment for her to realize it is Mr. Man just standing there.

She clutches her chest. "You scared me."

He says, "That was not my intent."

"Are you gonna go . . ." *To bed* sounds too odd to speak.

"No," he says.

She cannot discern his eyes in the darkness, just the perfectly proportioned outline of him. A pulse of unease starts at the base of her brain stem. But she dismisses it. Mr. Man has been wonderful, and besides, as the N0RM LLC slogan states, she is in charge.

"Thank you for cleaning up."

He is perfectly immobile, no tic, sway, or tremor. Of course, he has no need for tiny human movements. "You are welcome."

"Goodnight."

"Goodnight, Beccs."

Chapter 22

"I want to call a lawyer," Rebecca says at breakfast.

Eggs and waffles awaited them at the table this morning, courtesy of Mr. Man. Orange juice poured, vitamins set out, napkins folded. Wearing Mark's old jeans and a fresh black T-shirt, Mr. Man is cleaning out the refrigerator, checking dates and chucking past-due foods into a paper grocery bag.

Rebecca marvels at how quickly they have adjusted to having a full-time servant. It is lovely and yet also a touch disconcerting for reasons she cannot identify.

Mark shovels forkfuls into his mouth, eyes glued on his phone, thumbing through emails. It's annoying but she reminds herself to be happy to have him at breakfast. "Lawyers are expensive," he says. "There's zero proof of anything. And besides, that's exactly what Jackson wants."

"To get sued?"

"To cause more disruption and to substantiate his aggrieved victim status."

Maddy's eyes widen with curiosity, that wonderful openness Rebecca hopes the world will never dim. "What's *sued*, Mommy?"

"It's what you do to people who take advantage of you."

"Can I sue Sydney?"

Mark finally looks up with a laugh. He ruffles Maddy's hair. "I wish we could sue folks just for being a-holes, kiddo."

"Why? Who would *you* want to sue, Daddy?"

"Hmm." Mark sits back, folds his arms, taps his fingers, villain-like, on his biceps. "I like this game. If there was any one person I could sue for going out of his way to make my life miserable? Derek de Grasse."

"Your boss?"

"Not just a boss," Rebecca says. "Founder, CEO, thought leader, and visionary."

Mark cracks his sideways grin, the one that tugs his mouth to the left. "Yes. I wouldn't mind suing him to death."

"*I'd* like to sue Jackson into the ground," Rebecca says. "And sue Sydney's mom right in the face."

Maddy and Mark laugh.

All of a sudden, Mr. Man stands before them, holding a hunk of Stilton with the cellophane wrap peeled back, exposing a few blue veins. "Is this rotten?"

Mark and Rebecca look at each other, amused. The pungency wafting over the aroma of maple syrup makes it a fair question.

"No," Mark says. "That's just cheese. Cheese is mold."

"Mold is rotten."

"Sometimes. Sometimes it's just cheese."

"Oh. I will update my understanding." Mr. Man returns the Stilton to the fridge.

Mark shoves in a parting mouthful, checks his watch. Rising, he stops at the desk to sign the parent attendance slip for back-to-school night, as Maddy has reminded them to do a half dozen times. "Gotta run."

"Daddy Carpool?"

Mark is already out the door. "Sorry, kiddo, gotta get to the office."

Maddy runs the tines of her fork through the maple syrup. "Can Mr. Man take me to school, Mommy? Can he?"

It would be nice. Rebecca thinks about a warm bath, catching up on stockpiled *Grey's Anatomy* episodes, maybe even a workout. She feels a pang of guilt, but still, she does so much for everyone else all the time.

Maddy sets down her fork, dips her sticky fingers in her water glass, wipes them off repetitively on the napkin. She is rocking slightly. Watching her, Rebecca thinks about all the things she does every minute of every day to keep her daughter's beautiful little soul on track.

Doesn't she deserve a little time for herself?

She glances at Mr. Man and then at her daughter. "Sure thing, Maddy."

Chapter 23

The sun across Rebecca's face is so pleasing. The straps of the lawn chair press into her back, the Christmas tang of pine filling her lungs. Even with her eyes closed, she can sense the shadows of the bobbing branches playing across her eyelids.

When was the last time she came out to the front yard and just *sat*?

It is glorious.

She opens her eyes and notes with no small measure of satisfaction that the breeze is drizzling pine needles across Jackson's roof.

Two blocks up, a black BMW turns onto the street, and she feels a stab of anxiety.

Rising quickly, she hustles inside before he can spot her.

Chapter 24

As Rebecca pulls into the parking lot for pickup, Maddy skips to the minivan, backpack bouncing on her shoulders. Rebecca cannot remember the last time she's seen her daughter leave school wearing a smile.

Rebecca hits the button on the console and the side door slides open. Maddy flings her backpack before her, hops in, and buckles up. Another poke of the button and the door hums shut.

How touch-button easy everything has become, Rebecca thinks. Making espresso, dimming lights from the couch, sending payments.

"Guess what, Mommy? Sydney? She was actually nice, like *nice* nice, and she asked how my owie was and she meant it and no one even laughed. And they left me alone at lunch time."

How little it takes for this child to be happy. A few kind words, a modicum of care, being left to eat unmolested. Rebecca's heart breaks as it does a thousand times a day, but she reconstitutes it quietly.

"What do you say we do . . . Mommy-and-Maddy dinner?"

"Sushi rolls?"

"Yes, ma'am, we can do sushi rolls."

"I only want salmon, though."

"I wouldn't *dream* of making you eat anything other than salmon," Rebecca says, tapping on her signal and pulling out.

"Know who else eats salmon?"

Rebecca makes a claw hand, reaches back to scour the air. *"Raaar!"*

"Yup." Maddy giggles. "Grizzly bears."

Chapter 25

Singing along to *Hamilton* at the top of their lungs, they are badly out of key, which is the only way Rebecca can sing. Since there were no chores to get home to, Rebecca brought Maddy to the mall after dinner to get frozen yogurt, and even got them matching heart necklaces, which they now wear as a celebratory punctuation to the evening. Turning onto their street, Rebecca spots the flashing emergency lights, and her stomach drops through the bottom of her seat.

Fighting through shock, she notes the ambulance and cop cars are not at their house but next door.

"Mommy, what's happening?"

"I don't know. Looks like something's wrong at Jackson's house."

"Did someone sue him into the ground?"

But she cannot answer. The strobing blues and reds bring her back to the last time an ambulance came to their block. She remembers vividly being jangled around in the rear as they drove her off, the wand pressing through the cool ultrasound gel on her belly, the terrible sound of just one beating heart inside her.

She eases up to the curb in front of Jackson's. EMTs are pacing around, on their radios, looking grave. The cops are in a loose semicircle, standing guard over something. Through the bodies and vehicles, she notices a toppled ladder but can't make out anything else.

"Maddysaurus, wait in here, okay?"

The nickname slips out, but Maddy does not object.

Rebecca parks and unbuckles, sliding out. Neighbors are at their windows, making calls, filming on iPhones.

"Hello, hi?" Rebecca says, approaching. "Is everything okay?"

"Are you the wife?" a cop asks.

"Oh, thank God," an EMT says. "We got his wife!"

"No, I'm not his—"

But already she is being ushered forward into the inner sanctum. At first she struggles to register what is lying on the ground. It isn't shaped like a man, but a collection of wrong angles.

Jackson lies grotesquely contorted, limbs bent this way and that, his head at an unnatural tilt on his neck. But that isn't the worst part.

The worst part is that he is staring straight up at her.

He blinks rapidly. A line of drool runs down the side of his cheek.

Her breath catches in her throat, and she has to try twice before she can unstick it.

"He's in bad shape," the EMT says. "Do you want to say anything to him?"

Rebecca finally locates her voice. "I'm not his wife. I'm just . . . just the neighbor."

Jackson glares up at her. One cheek is mashed to the earth, the visible eye bloodshot and bulging. Spittle flecks his lips. His lower lip quivers. He is irreversibly shattered in so many ways, like a car-struck dog that must be put down.

Rebecca can hardly make out anything over the rush of white noise in her ears. Her heart thumps against her ribs, fluttering her sweater. She's amazed everyone else doesn't hear it too.

She is clutching herself across her stomach, one hand clawing at her neck. She feels a tug—the necklace giving way?—but she cannot move her gaze from Jackson. It's like he is impaling her with that one eye.

And he looks angry. No, not angry. *Accusatory.*

He tries to speak, but all that comes out is a garbled mess. That continuous cord of drool keeps spilling from his lips.

"Help him," she hears herself say. "Why aren't you helping him?"

"We've stabilized him as best we can," the EMT says. "But we need a full-blown paramedic here. No way we're risking snapping that neck entirely."

"He's paralyzed for sure, man," one of the young cops says too loudly. "For sure."

Rebecca thinks, *He can hear you.*

But at the same time, Jackson seems gone already, less a man than the remnants of an accident. Given his state, she wonders what, if anything, he can take in. The scream of a siren splits the air, more help arriving, but still she cannot tear her gaze from that hideous eye.

It twitches in the socket, pinning her.

"*Errug,*" Jackson says. And then, an agonized roar. "*Eeruuggh!*"

Horrified, she stumbles back.

Tripping, falling onto the fresh-cut lawn, shoving up from hands and knees. The colossal fire engine seems to fill the entire world, flying up to the curb behind her van. Maddy is gone from the back seat and Rebecca's panic revs higher into redline, but as she whips her gaze up the street, she sees Mr. Man ushering Maddy in through their front door, one smooth hand at the side of her head to block her view of the accident.

Paramedics and firemen spill out, storming past Rebecca as she staggers to her van. Her hands tremble so badly she almost cannot fit the key into the slot.

She drives crookedly into the driveway, banging across the curb, and manages to slot the van into the garage without crashing.

She takes a moment to gather herself before entering the house.

Maddy is at the table, the calming scent of Nervous Tummy Tea rising from the mug before her, permeating the kitchen. She is smiling and talking with Mr. Man.

"They are from Africa," she is saying. "Rhodesia, which is now called Zimbobby."

"Zimbabwe," Mr. Man says, moving clean plates from dishwasher to cupboard.

"Zimbobby," Maddy says again. "And they were bred to hunt lions. *Raaar!*" She makes raaar claws just as Rebecca did earlier, her pug nose scrunched up in a snarl. She notices Rebecca standing there. "You okay, Mommy?"

"Yeah, Maddysaurus. I'm okay. It's just . . . Jackson had an accident."

"A accident? He cut his finger?"

"No, honey," Rebecca says. "He fell off his ladder."

"Owie!"

"Yeah." Rebecca is still trying to breathe normally. "Owie."

"He gonna be awright, Mommy?"

The pause is quiet enough that she can hear Bao-Bao nibbling at his water nozzle.

"I hope so."

"I'll say a prayer for him."

"That'd be nice, Maddysaurus."

Maddy's eyelids are heavy, her blinks long; she is crashing from the Froyo sugar high. Rebecca rests a hand on Maddy's head, surprised as always by how warm it is. Maddy gets up, and Rebecca keeps her palm atop her sweaty hair, steering her down the hall to her bedroom.

They skip bath, and the rest of the nigh-night routine goes swiftly and smoothly until it is time for forehead kiss.

Maddy pokes a finger at the hollow of Rebecca's throat. "Where's your necklace, Mommy?"

Memory flash: Rebecca standing over Jackson's buckled form, clawing at her neck, the give of the cheap filament chain.

"Oh," she says. "I know where I left it."

"Better go get it," Maddy says, so sleepy the last words come out as one: *geddit*. "So we can be twinsies tomorrow."

And she is asleep.

As Rebecca pads down the hall, she rubs her shoulder, which has abruptly knotted. Mr. Man stands in the sparkling kitchen, sponge in hand, everything polished to a shine. Not a crumb, not a smudge. Maddy's lunch box has been retrieved from the minivan, cleaned, and left open face down to dry on a dish towel.

Rebecca smacks her forehead. "Groceries. I forgot to get groceries."

"Are you hungry?" Mr. Man asks.

"No, no, we ate. Just need to make her lunch for tomorrow. Can you rustle something up? Something fresh and healthy?"

"Of course," Mr. Man says.

"Okay. Be right back. I left something next door."

As she exits the house and steps clear of the porch, the sudden quiet of the neighborhood cocoons her. The fire engine is gone, as are the cop cars and ambulance. A few bits of trash wag in the breeze on Jackson's lawn—a square of gauze, a wrapper from some medical implement, scissored-off shreds of clothing. His house is dark.

The ladder remains there on its side, ominous in the moonlight. How little it takes for a life to be immutably altered. A visit to a developmental pediatrician, a placental abnormality, a toppled ladder.

As she cuts through the break in the hedge, she holds her gaze steady on the fallen ladder. Tentatively she approaches the spot where Jackson landed. Several spots in the dirt are soaked dark. It is hard to look away from them.

It feels odd to be standing here on Jackson's side of the divide. Aside from this evening, she has never been over here.

A light rain starts up, spitting at her cheeks. She steps up onto his porch for cover and to get a better vantage, hoping to spot a sparkle of plated silver in the grass.

The soles of her shoes stick to the poured concrete. Jackson's porch is gummed up with sap from her pine tree. It's a lot.

In fact, it's quite awful.

Leaning out from the eaves, she gazes up at the gutters. Their edges, too, are caked with sap, bristling with pine needles.

She feels like a total asshole. How different the perspective is. Here across the hedge, the pine tree isn't a source of pride but a shedding mess.

The rain quickens, a snare drum rat-a-tat-tatting against the roof.

As she lowers her gaze, she catches a glimmer among the blades of grass. There it is, her cheap half-a-heart pendant. Gathering it up, she hurries home. The moon is almost full, the light nearly orange. She notes the fine patterns of needles on the ground.

She reaches the break in the hedge.

For a moment, she does not believe her eyes. The humming has returned, a bee swarm filling her head. Her nerves are tingling, all of them, all at once.

Pressed into the wet dirt of the gap in the hedge, a single barefoot print.

The toes slightly too proportional.

They are aimed in the direction of Jackson's house.

Forgetting to breathe, she watches as the raindrops pick apart the faint impression, melting it back into the mud.

Chapter 26

As Rebecca walks up the front path, her stomach roils with trepidation. Alexa de Grasse's words echo uninvited in her mind: *It'll see to everything you* really *want. In your darkest heart of hearts.* What the hell does that mean? This isn't what Rebecca wants. She doesn't even know what she wants.

Overhead the pine tree whispers and sways, a tangled mass of shadow. Her legs don't tremble, but they feel numb, bloodless. The thought of Maddy inside with *him* drives her forward onto the porch, through the front door, into the kitchen.

Mr. Man stands near the sink, back turned, his arm working at something. As she nears, she sees that Bao-Bao is on the counter, but it isn't Bao-Bao.

It's a puddle of a rabbit, skinned cleanly as if in a single go.

Her vision sparkles with static and she is still drifting forward as if in a dream and she comes around Mr. Man's sawing elbow and sees the butcher knife and the fascia-sheathed meat, the skeins of vessel and fiber. Her stomach lurches and she shoulders him aside and vomits three times, neatly, into the sink.

Running the faucet, the disposal, she arms sweat-pasted hair off her forehead. "What did you do?" she asks dumbly. "What did you do?"

He looks up, the knife in his hand edged with a rippled stripe of crimson. "You said fresh and healthy. It was the only item in the kitchen that resembles real food."

Her voice comes as a hoarse whisper, the back of her throat scorched with stomach acid: "Not food. A *pet*. A beloved pet."

His eyes flare, a simulation of empathy. "Oh. I am sorry."

She nods, tries to speak, fails.

"I will update my understanding."

A breath screeches inward. "My God. What am I gonna tell Maddy? What am I gonna . . . ?"

Mr. Man sets down the knife and moves toward her comfortingly. "Would you like me to take care of this?"

She recoils. "Just—*go*. Please go."

He steps away from her. Starts out of the kitchen.

The colorful mess on the counter stabs at her peripheral vision. "Wait. Clean this up. Clean this up, and then . . ." Her flat palm is up, facing out, a stop sign between them.

Mr. Man gets to work, bundling what is left of Bao-Bao into a trash bag. Then he wipes the counter and cleans the knife, setting it out to dry.

He walks out of the house, trash bag dangling from his fist.

The instant Rebecca hears the front door close, she races up the hall, flying into Maddy's bedroom. Maddy is happily asleep, snuggled between Mr. Fox and Mr. Elephant.

Rebecca stands in the dark of the bedroom, breathing hard, stars from Sleeptime Pillow Pet projected across the walls, the ceiling, her body.

Withdrawing, she strides down the hall.

Mr. Man is not in the nursery.

He is not in the kitchen.

He is not in the backyard.

The front door is still unlocked. From the porch, she can see the too-full trash bins at the curb, the edge of Bao-Bao's burial trash bag peeking from beneath the cover.

Mark. She has to call Mark.

He picks up right away, but she doesn't wait for him to say anything, her words rushing out of her: "Mark, Mark—get home *now*."

Chapter 27

Mark's hands are shaking so hard he can't set down his umpteenth cup of coffee on his desk without spilling. He hates hearing Rebecca's voice like that, when it spikes into rawness. Stuffing his laptop into his briefcase, he shoves out of his office into the corridor.

At the end of the hall, Derek's light is still on. Through the interior window Mark sees Derek with his head lowered, speaking into the phone, lifting his jacket from the back of his Aeron.

Mark's breath snags in his throat.

He withdraws into his office, closes the door, sits back down at his desk, pretending to review papers.

Hiding like a child.

A few moments later, Derek's words come audible, the phone argument rising in pitch like the whine of an approaching car engine: ". . . root causes," he is saying, "we need to identify root causes. I want immediate, actionable steps based on the forecasting . . ."

His shadow flickers by Mark's office, his footsteps fading. Finally Mark hears the ding of the elevator arriving.

After a few seconds, Mark emerges like prey from a burrow, head craning, blinking into the fluorescents.

Down the same hall, following Derek's footsteps on a delay, his mouth dry.

Bao-Bao has been skinned and Jackson has fallen off a ladder and Rebecca said something about a footprint. Mark couldn't clarify the details, but it all sounded ominous as hell. It has been mounting, whatever this is. Lately, when he sees Rebecca's name on his caller ID, dread stirs his gut as it had in those endless days after the miscarriage when he'd felt his cortisol spike every time the phone rang.

He rides the elevator down in silence, nervously knocking his briefcase against the side of his thigh. When the doors peel open, he spots Derek's Porsche whipping past and he flattens himself against the elevator buttons to hide from view.

His face burns. The family pet has been killed and his wife is terrified and here he is, hiding from his boss in an elevator.

The 911 gives a throaty roar as it banks up the ramp. From Derek's braggadocio, Mark knows that the engine is 518 horsepower, the model a GT3 RS.

It whips out of view, and Mark scurries from the elevator to his car.

Chapter 28

The titanium business card is out on the tiny kitchen desk. Mark is pounding away at his laptop, and Rebecca is pacing tight circles, working the phone. They have a website, an email, and a 1-800 number for N0RM LLC. But they cannot reach a live person.

The customer service is run by AI chatbots, infuriating in their lack of emotional responsiveness. Mark should know; this is precisely what he spends his days at the office doing, replacing human beings with artificial intelligence. And now he is reaping the whirlwind.

I'm sorry we cannot respond right now, the interface coolly informs him. We can schedule a time for you to talk to your Experience Facilitator during business hours.

He and Rebecca have been at this for hours, discussing, plotting, processing, venting, attempting contact.

"This can't wait until tomorrow!" Rebecca hisses into the phone, her conversation mirroring his typed interface. A vein is lifted at her temple, a snarl of hair pasted across her forehead. She curses, taps the phone onto speaker, pushes buttons at intervals, navigating the interface.

"For sales, press 1."

"For billing, press 2."

"For an Experience Facilitator, press 3."

Rebecca finger-slaps the iPhone. "I already did this!"

"They're closed, Beccs."

"I thought the founder was South African or whatever. Isn't it daytime in Africa?"

"We're sorry, but our Facilitation Center is not open. Please try back during business hours."

"But the business is based here," Mark tells her. "It's a 1-800 number."

"For sales, press 1."

"Fuck you," Rebecca tells the phone. "Fuck. You."

She hangs up.

Their website is slow loading so Mark hits refresh on the pop-up window.

. . .

Would you like to schedule a time to talk to
your Experience Facilitator this week?

Angrily he types: Tomorrow.

> Luca is available tomorrow at 6 pm Pacific Standard Time.

Mark types: Earlier.

> We are sorry. That is the first available time slot.

He clicks to accept, slams the laptop lid down, bangs a fist on the desk.

The titanium card pops up, flips over, lands on its back: **YOU'RE IN CHARGE.**

They stare at the words.

"Not so much," Rebecca says.

"Okay, okay," Mark says, trying to reset. "Let's not overreact."

"A robot-man butchered Maddy's pet on my counter and might've broken Jackson's neck."

"We've been over this, Beccs. We don't know that he did anything to Jackson—"

"No? He went over there to borrow a cup of sugar?"

"We don't know he went over there."

"There was a footprint. *His* footprint."

"*Maybe* his. And now it's gone."

"No. Don't do that. Do *not* do that. I saw it, Mark. Don't you gaslight me."

"I'm not gaslighting you. I'm just saying, you are—*we* are—understandably in an anxiety spin cycle. We'd do well to slow down, take a breath."

"Tell it to Bao-Bao."

"I get it," he says. "And it's awful. Completely awful. He doesn't understand things, like when he didn't get that the cheese wasn't rotten."

"This isn't cheese, Mark!"

"I agree that he—it—this—is dangerous. I'm just saying it's a mix-up, not necessarily malicious. AI gets screwy sometimes, hallucinates responses. It's an interface problem. I deal with them at work all the time."

"Is our paralyzed neighbor an 'interface problem'?" She throws air quotes.

"Beccs, if there was a footprint—"

"There *was* a footprint."

"—he could've gone over there for a bunch of reasons. Why would he want to hurt Jackson?"

She doesn't want to say it out loud. Saying the words makes it more real. She musters her courage. "I said I wished I could sue him into the ground."

"Oh, come on, Beccs. That was a joke. It doesn't mean you wanted Mr. Man to—to take some vigilante action."

"He doesn't understand things," Rebecca says bitingly. "Like the cheese."

Mark draws in a deep breath. He rubs his face. When he lowers his hands, he looks pale, diminished.

"We don't even know where he is," Rebecca says.

"At least he's not here. I don't want that thing in the house."

That's when they hear the click of a latch, the twist of the front doorknob.

They freeze.

They hear a footstep.

Another.

Mark is wedged into the tiny desk. Slowly he rolls the cheap white IKEA chair out, swings his legs free. Rebecca backs up very slowly until her lumbar hits the counter.

More footfall.

They wait, forgetting to breathe.

At last a shadow falls through the open doorway.

And then Mr. Man appears.

Cradled in his arms is a Mini Lop bunny.

"Here is a replacement bunny," Mr. Man says. "Just like Bao-Bao."

The rabbit has Bao-Bao's coloring and seems to be around six pounds. In fact, he looks remarkably like the original Bao-Bao.

Mr. Man walks calmly across the kitchen, squats, and eases the bunny into Bao-Bao's cage. Then he stands up to face them.

Mark and Rebecca have not moved an inch.

Mr. Man says, "I took care of it for you."

"Where did you—" Mark's voice gutters dryly. He swallows with effort and begins again: "Where did you get a Mini Lop rabbit at"—quick check of his watch—"four in the morning?"

"Your breeder, Ginny Merchant," Mr. Man says. "She has several litters."

"You woke her up?"

"There was no need. There are several rabbit hutches in her backyard. I did not want to disrupt her sleep and potentially alarm her. My value hierarchy ranks her ease of mind higher than immediate payment. I reimbursed her through your PayPal, link to bank account number 8179—"

"Jesus," Mark says. "Jesus Christ."

When she trusts her voice again, Rebecca says, "You can't just break into someone's backyard and steal a pet."

"I did not steal the rabbit. I paid for the rabbit."

"That's not how it works," Rebecca says. "That's illegal."

"My value hierarchy ranks your and Maddy's happiness higher."

Silence fills the kitchen.

"Higher than *what*?" Rebecca finally asks.

Mr. Man's eyes dim. He closes them, chin dipping, lids flickering. He opens his eyes, lifts his head sluggishly. "My power level is low. I must recharge."

He moves jerkily across the kitchen, as if running out of steam.

"Wait," Rebecca says.

Mr. Man halts. His head droops slightly on his neck.

Her voice shakes: "Did you go over to Jackson's last night?"

"Yes," Mr. Man says.

Rebecca tries to swallow, but her throat will not comply. She forces out the question: "Why?"

Mr. Man stares at her, unblinking. Mark is on his feet beside her. They stand rib to rib. They wait.

"I saw your necklace break," Mr. Man says. "I went to search for it."

Relief washes through Rebecca. She exhales through clenched teeth. She wants to believe that so badly, and she mostly does. Maybe it *is* the truth. Maybe that's when Mr. Man left the footprint, after the fact.

Mr. Man starts himself up again, seemingly stiff from his low charge. As soon as he clears the threshold to the foyer, Mark and Rebecca look at each other. "Maddy," they say in unison.

They lean into the hall in time to see Mr. Man disappear into the nursery.

Down the hall together, taking quiet steps.

They arrive at the doorway. The clamshell lid is lowering with a faint hum, the sound more electronic than mechanical. They stand and watch until the coffin-like prism is closed. The sensor light comes on.

Mark walks over, checks the seal. Rebecca sets her hands on the closed lid.

It is shut as tight as a walnut.

Mark shoves it, but it is so heavy it doesn't budge.

"I'll sleep on the floor in Maddy's room," he says. "In case he wakes up. I don't want him unsupervised until we can get him returned."

Rebecca nods.

They start out, and Mark walks her to the bedroom door. They embrace. It feels good, warm and familiar. On his neck she can smell a trace of that sage-and-cedar soap.

They pull apart. "We'll figure this out," Mark says. "It's late, and I'm mostly certain we're overreacting."

She nods. He is probably right. What happened to Bao-Bao is terrible, but Mr. Man set it right, and the footprint doesn't prove anything.

She gives him a kiss, starts into the bedroom.

He catches her by the biceps. "Lock the door anyway," he says.

Chapter 29

Black smudges mar the pouches beneath Mark's eyes, and he looks gaunt with stress and lack of sleep. Rebecca looks even worse.

It is 6:30 a.m.

Mark sits on Maddy's bed, thumbing away at his phone while Rebecca gets Maddy ready for school in the bathroom, making sure she remembers to brush her molars.

"Wha ids Dabby ind hebe?" Maddy says through a mouthful of toothpaste.

Rebecca tries at a translation: "Why is Daddy in here?"

Maddy nods, leaning forward, a pointy beard of Crest froth dangling from her chin. She washes her face clean.

"He just wants to see you."

"But he isn't seeing me. He's on his phone. Like always."

"He's just digging out from work, Maddysaurus. There's been a lot going on."

But when Rebecca peers into the bedroom, Mark is not on his phone anymore. Instead he is leafing through a photo album of Maddy's birth, which he has pulled off the bookshelf. The photo on the cover is Rebecca way pregnant, hand on her belly, smiling at the iPhone. The iOS photo software selected the best pictures from the avalanche they took in the first months, a one-click companion app outsourced them, and three days later the album showed up, manufactured in Vietnam. The pictures are the best ones, she supposes, but the album itself feels generic, devoid of warmth, stamped out of a mold. She misses the yellowed edges of photographs from her youth, the sticky cellophane that trapped them imperfectly in place against the album pages.

Mark flips through the images of their family's genesis, his face soft, thoughtful. Affection stirs in Rebecca's chest as she watches him, a young-feeling love from when they were first dating, first pregnancy, when it was the two of them side by side embarking on their adventure in the world.

The sound of dishes clanking in the kitchen disrupts her reverie. Mark's head snaps up. The last they checked, Mr. Man was still sealed in his prism, recharging.

Mark takes a breath, nods at her reassuringly.

After Maddy dresses and loads her backpack, the three-some head down the hall, Mark in the lead.

Mr. Man stands over the table, holding a pot of fresh coffee. Scrambled eggs steam on plates. Forks rest on napkins, including Maddy's with the watermelon handle.

Mark and Rebecca stare at Mr. Man.

He looks innocuous, helpful, the Mr. Man they knew before.

"Would you like coffee?" Mr. Man says. "Kenyan blend?"

Mark says, "Sure."

Mr. Man pours two cups.

Rebecca and Mark are still standing across the room, Maddy behind them, chewing on a backpack strap. Over on the kitchen desk, the titanium business card winks in the morning sun.

The toaster pops, and Rebecca, on edge, gives a little yelp.

Mr. Man retrieves the toast with bare fingers, resilient to the heat, and lays a slice on each plate. That breaks the spell.

As Mark and Rebecca sit, Maddy dashes over to the rabbit cage. "Morning, Bao-Bao!"

She unlatches the cage and gathers the bunny into her arms, stroking his neck.

Rebecca says, "Mr. Man, why don't you rake the pine needles in the front yard?"

Mr. Man gives a tidy little bow and exits through the garage, where the gardening tools are kept.

Mark sets his iPhone on the table, presses to dial, hits Speaker.

"Mommy," Maddy says.

Rebecca hushes her, points to Mark's phone. The speaker announces ringing on the other end of the call.

Derek answers by saying, "Tell me you updated the readability enhancements on the bot modules."

"I have," Mark says in a strained voice. "But I'll have to send them from home."

"Why's that?" Derek makes no effort to disguise his aggravation.

"I have strep," Mark lies.

"Strep," Derek says suspiciously.

Maddy is regarding "Bao-Bao" differently. "*Mommy,*" she says in a strained whisper.

Rebecca puts a hush finger to her lips.

"Yeah," Mark says. "It's going around Maddy's school."

"Kids are petri dishes," Derek says. "Send the update. And get antibiotics or whatever. I need you back here ASAP."

Derek cuts the line.

Mark rubs his face. When he's done, Rebecca catches his eye, mouths, *Thank you.*

"Daddy, you have strep?"

"I'm not feeling so good, kiddo. I might have to get a test."

"But you said you *had* strep."

"I know, Maddysaurus. I might."

"Why don't I get you to school," Rebecca says, "so Daddy can stay here and rest?"

Maddy feeds "Bao-Bao" back into the crate, comes to the table, picks at her eggs. "What's for lunch?"

"I didn't have time to make lunch," Rebecca says. "So you'll have to buy today."

"I hate buying."

"I know."

"'Less it's grilled-cheese day."

"I know."

Maddy scampers to the fridge, checks the printout. "It's not grilled-cheese day."

"I know."

Maddy screws up her face. "It's fish sticks. They're super gross. And I hate waiting in line. And having to figure out change. If I don't get it right, the other kids make fun of me."

Rebecca crosses the kitchen and leans to see out the bay windows. Mr. Man is raking the front yard. He'll be at it a long time, and then Mark will find other chores to keep him busy until the six o'clock call with N0RM LLC.

"You'll get it right," she hears Mark say. "It's just math. And besides, the other kids are being nicer, right?"

And then Maddy: "It won't last."

Rebecca wonders if there will come a day when one of Maddy's simple observations won't shatter her heart. When she turns around, Maddy darts over to her. "Mommy. I've been trying to tell you." She points. "That's not Bao-Bao."

Rebecca grapples with opening this fresh can of worms right now in the middle of everything else. She yearns to give way to the truth, but if she does there will be a world-ending meltdown and more emotions and complications, and she cannot contend with more emotions and complications in this moment. She feels a frozen weight across her face, heavy like a mask.

She hears herself saying, "Sure it is, Maddysaurus."

Mark steps in: "Off you go, kiddo. You're gonna be late."

Maddy grabs her backpack and scampers into the garage, Rebecca trailing.

Mark looks up. "We got this," he tells her.

Rebecca swallows past the lump in her throat.

Chapter 30

On the drive to school, Rebecca plays the Disney Channel on Sirius, hoping to forestall conversation. Maddy mouths the words listlessly, staring out the window, troubled.

Rebecca checks the clock, inching its way forward. She just has to get to 6:00 p.m. Then they will have answers and options. Plugged into the dashboard, her phone dings and chimes with notifications, oblivious as always to the emotional stakes of the moment. Text-to-speech spits out a bureaucratic assault—a missed package delivery requiring signature, a broken water meter that needs repair, phase three of an endless disputing process regarding inaccurate bills from selfsame broken water meter.

Distracted, she almost clips a bright-red Jaguar SUV pulling into the kiss-and-ride line. The driver slams the horn with the heel of her hand. Rebecca waves an apology, her mortification growing when she sees Sydney's mom, Sheila, behind the wheel.

Sheila recognizes Rebecca, her face ripple-transforming into a practiced expression of affability. But her cheeks are too defined, her eyes feline sharp.

When it's time to lurch forward in the line, Sheila flares her manicured hand, making a point of waving Rebecca ahead of her. Face burning, Rebecca gives a nervous gesture of thanks.

She pulls up to the drop-off point and taps the button for the minivan door to slide open.

But Maddy hits the button, and the door jerks shut again.

"*Mommy,*" she says.

"Time to go, Maddysaurus." To Rebecca's own ears, her voice sounds chirpy and fake. It sounds like the kind of voice Sheila Evans would use. "Let's not hold up the line."

But Maddy scrambles forward, leaning past the console to whisper hotly in Rebecca's ear. "Bao-Bao isn't Bao-Bao. Someone *replaced* him."

Behind them, a horn blares. In the rearview, Rebecca sees Sheila give a lipsticked grin and a semi-aggressive wave for her to move along.

"No one replaced Bao-Bao," Rebecca says on autopilot. She has long prided herself on her honesty, and yet now when it matters most, how easily she lies, how quickly it comes. "Don't be silly, Maddysaurus."

Maddy stays leaning forward, her backpack crowding the ceiling of the van, looking at her mom. Her expression is confusion and dismay. "I said, don't *call me* that!"

The horn sounds again, and then another, a chorus of impatience.

"You have to get out, honey," Rebecca says.

Maddy gives her a bruised look and slides toward the rear, tugged by the weight of her backpack. Rebecca glances back. Maddy's brow is furrowed the way it gets when she talks about Sydney and the Mean Girls.

She looks betrayed.

Because she has been.

Patrick, a kiss-and-ride mainstay, helps gather Maddy out of the minivan and then knocks semi-aggressively on the side panel for Rebecca to get moving.

Rebecca pulls out.

In the rearview she watches Sheila shaking her head, rolling her eyes at one of the mom volunteers through the window.

Rebecca drives several blocks toward home.

Signaling responsibly, she pulls the minivan over to the curb.

She hears Maddy in her head, the scared whisper: *Bao-Bao isn't Bao-Bao*. Then she replays herself gaslighting her daughter: *Don't be silly, Maddysaurus*.

What is happening to her? What is she doing?

Her breaths jerk quicker and quicker until she lowers her face into her hands and sobs.

Chapter 31

"We have a no-return policy," Luca tells Rebecca and Mark over Zoom.

Their officious Experience Facilitator is, as always, impeccably made up, smoky eyes and bloody lipstick. A black turtleneck furls beneath that clearly defined jawbone. Her hair is drawn back sharply enough to trace the perfectly smooth curve of her skull. In the superb lighting, her cheekbones are contoured. She is devastatingly beautiful.

If she is real.

Rebecca and Mark are huddled together on Maddy's bed, Mark's laptop open before them. Maddy plays on the interlocking foam tiles that form a play area on her floor. She snaps together one of her Lego 3-in-1s, transitioning it from bald eagle to scorpion. To diminish sensory overload, she wears pink padded noise-canceling headphones. Chewing her bottom lip, she is entranced in the work of building, her fingers deft and confident. The softness of twilight through the slats lies across her face, her big expressive eyes so open, so vulnerable. With her unfiltered EQ, unfakeable kindness, and unquenchable curiosity, she is the purest being Rebecca has ever known.

For not the first time, Rebecca wonders if her daughter is the one who is autistic or if in fact the ones actually on the spectrum are all the so-called normal girls with their Snapchat streaks and numb expressions and social-hierarchy dominance games.

"What does that mean?" Mark says, "precisely?"

"Your payment is nonrefundable."

"That's fine." Rebecca keeps her voice low, even though Mr. Man has gone back into his prism to recharge for the night. "Can you just . . . take him?"

"He is highly customized. He was grown from you. There is no other use for him."

"I don't care," Mark says. "That's not our problem."

"We're uncomfortable with him now," Rebecca adds, her tone *can't we all just get along* conciliatory.

"Because he went to look for your necklace?"

"That's what he *said* he did. But as I explained, there was a—an accident. With our neighbor . . ."

"What are you suggesting?"

"He killed our rabbit," Mark says. "Skinned him for a meal."

Rebecca pats the air for him to quiet, her anxious gaze on Maddy, but Maddy continues constructing the scorpion's tail, her headphones snug. "Bao-Bao" is beside her on the mat, velvet ears poking up, nose quivering as he nibbles on a braided rope made of compressed timothy hay.

"Then you must have instructed him to do so," Luca says. "He is entirely an extension of you. Remember: You are in charge."

"I did *not* instruct him to do that," Rebecca says.

"You have explained that. You have explained that it was a misunderstanding. As we explained in the onboarding process, you must be clear about what you are asking and what you want."

"I *was* clear," Rebecca says. "Just please. Can you take him?" She hates that she sounds like she is pleading. She hates that she *is* pleading.

Mark addresses Luca or the Luca bot: "Are you saying you will not pick him back up?"

"That is not part of our legally binding contract."

"I can't imagine there will be good press on this," Mark says. "An unhappy family . . ." He lets the words hang.

Luca stares at them for a time, blinking at too-regular intervals, that perfect jaw set. "Are you threatening this corporation, Mr. Higgins?"

"No," Mark says, though of course he is trying to. "I'm saying that this isn't a great customer-service look for a new company."

More evenly spaced blinks as Luca processes. "I remind you that we have access to all your family's information."

Mark goes rigid on the mattress next to her. Even sitting beside him, Rebecca can feel his body temperature rise. Or maybe that's just hers.

"Are you threatening *us?*" Mark asks.

"Of course not. I am merely reminding you that this corporation and your family's interests are organically and digitally intertwined."

"I understand that," Rebecca says, still trying for amity. "But after what happened to our neighbor . . . What if he harmed him?"

"He did not harm anyone," Luca says. "Unless you wanted him to."

"I *didn't* want him to," Rebecca insists. "I don't want him to."

"Communicate with him clearly."

"It's not that easy."

"Yes. It is. You are doing it. Right now."

"What does that mean?"

There is a suspended moment. And then Rebecca sees Mark's eyes drop to regard his cell phone leerily. Rebecca follows his stare as it next pulls to the teddy bear nanny cam. She feels her own iPhone in her pocket, pressed into her thigh, its camera and microphone ever present. And she remembers that—of course—Mr. Man can hear and see all, even when his eyes are closed, even when he is locked in his electronic casket recharging. Her hand has crept over to find Mark's.

"He has access," Luca says, "to everything."

Horripilation creeps across Rebecca's flesh, tightening the skin at the small of her back, her nape, her hairline.

She senses heat like pressure on the side of her face. Even before she drags her gaze up, she knows with terrible certainty that something is watching her.

A man's backlit form stands in the open doorway of Maddy's bedroom.

Rebecca tries to scream but the sound is stifled in her throat. Her hand jerks in Mark's, and his knees jump, knocking the laptop from his lap. It bounces on Maddy's bed, snapping shut, terminating their chat.

She blinks, and Mr. Man is gone.

"What?" Mark is saying, but she can barely hear him over the thundering rush in her head. "What?"

"He was there." Rebecca's voice sounds strangled. "Watching us."

Mark slides off the bed, trying to let go of her hand, but she holds on, rising with him.

Maddy continues on with her scorpion, oblivious beneath the pink headphones. When she is focused, her concentration is unbreakable.

Mark leads out of the bedroom and down the hall.

The nursery door is open.

The lights are off.

The lid of the prism is raised.

Mr. Man waits in the darkness, standing by the closet.

He raises his arms wide above his head, a predatory display.

Rebecca yelps, jumping behind Mark. They tense, bracing for attack.

But it is not a show of aggression.

Mr. Man is stretching.

Next he does deep knee bends, the movement brisk, muscular. He is loosening his body up from his time in the prism.

"Maybe you should go back in." Mark's voice is dry, feeble. "Keep recharging."

They wait for a response until it becomes clear that no response is forthcoming.

Mr. Man laces his fingers together and twist-thrusts his hands outward. There is a cracking of joints or whatever it is that Mr. Man has. The precision of his motions betrays just how powerful he is.

For the first time, Rebecca fully comprehends what they have done, that they have invited something with full-grown-man strength to live under their roof.

Mr. Man takes a high grip on the bathroom doorjamb and wings his arm back, opening his shoulder and chest on one side and then the other, each flicker of movement uncannily precise.

Mark and Rebecca steal a look at each other. What the hell are they supposed to do?

Rebecca steps out from behind Mark. "Look, I know you overheard our conversation with Luca . . ."

Mr. Man's head swivels over to her. In the darkness of the bedroom, his features are not visible. There is only a black oval where his face should be. He is still stretching, pulling his shoulder blades back, together, but his head remains completely motionless, the effect deeply unsettling.

Her voice wobbles, almost fails: "I think we'd do well to take a break. Wouldn't you like to take a break too?"

"No." Mr. Man arches backward, flexing his lumbar. "I would not."

"We'd like you to get back into the prism," Mark says. His tone is tough, but Rebecca can sense the fear beneath it, and she knows that Mr. Man can as well.

Mr. Man stops stretching, statue still. He seems like something carved from wood, a totem pole.

Rebecca's muscles are tight enough to cramp. Her calves, hip flexors, the side of her neck—everything aches. She feels coiled, ready to flee if Mr. Man springs at them, which it seems he will at any moment. Menace rolls off him, tangible enough to choke on. She cannot find enough oxygen, can't manage to draw in a full breath.

When Mr. Man speaks, his voice comes as a lifeless monotone: "I have more to take care of for you."

A scream shatters the silence—Maddy. A deep, pained cry of anguish.

Rebecca's body moves before her brain catches up. She is running up the hall, bare feet pounding the tiles, Mark behind her.

She bursts into Maddy's bedroom and sees Maddy backed all the way to the toy bin rack, her finger shoved in her mouth. She stares wild-eyed at "Bao-Bao," who sits in the middle of the foam play area, marble eyed and innocent. The Lego giraffe lies in pieces, trampled.

"He bit me," Maddy shrieks. "He bit my finger."

The cries shuddering out of her are unadulterated, pure sorrow. She cannot comprehend that this has happened to her.

Rebecca moves to her, arms spread, but Maddy closes her eyes and stamps her feet; touch will send her further into the abyss. Her headphones have fallen around her neck.

On her knees, Rebecca makes soothing noises, and finally Maddy relents and tumbles into her, arms thrown weakly around her neck, hot face pressed to her cheek.

"I don't know why he bit me," she says. "I don't know what I did."

"You didn't do anything, Maddysaurus. You didn't do anything at all."

Maddy pulls away, points at the rabbit. "Get him out of here," she says angrily. "Get him gone."

Rebecca scoops up the bunny. Mark is still in the doorway, breathing hard. He steps backward, peers down the hall.

Mr. Man. They have forgotten about Mr. Man.

"We'll take care of Bao-Bao," Rebecca tells Maddy. "You put Mr. Giraffe back together."

Maddy screws a fist into her eye socket like a much younger child than she is. She nods.

Holding not-Bao-Bao tight to her chest, Rebecca hurries down the hall with Mark.

In the nursery, the prism lid is lifted.

The casket is empty.

And Mr. Man is nowhere to be seen.

Chapter 32

When Derek is this pissed off at the world, he requires garage time. He is not a fan of the so-called man caves permeating the cultural conversation. He doesn't need a cave. The whole house is—should be—his castle.

Given the less-than-buoyant stock performance and the underbidders nibbling away at his client base, he wonders how long he will be able to keep the house, or at least the toys he has accumulated. Like the lineup of vintage Porsches in the detached five-car garage he built along the south side of their lot. That's the thing with the tech sector—it's a constant battle to stay relevant, to maximize for efficiency and cost, to keep a quarter step ahead of the competition. A thoroughbred race with everyone riding tech that's smarter and more powerful than the humans who are allegedly steering it.

Derek's ire about the performance dip lands disproportionately on Mark, even though Mark is clearly the most talented of the chief product officers—maybe *because* Mark is the most talented. Derek expects more from him, just as he expects the most out of himself. It doesn't have to do with the fact that Alexa tried to make out with him once, or that Mark is stalwart in a way that Derek slightly envies.

The jungle of e-news is not for sissies. When it comes to content optimization, it's a wolf-eat-wolf world, a constantly changing, algorithmically powered process of evolutionary selection. Miss a step, and you're extinct.

And they've been missing a lot of steps lately.

That's why Derek needs to be out here to clear his head, away from the laptop that keeps him tethered to disappointing Nasdaq news and the endless complications of keeping a public company on track. Away from Alexa, too, and her incessant needs and drives. She is in the bedroom right now, enjoying their recharged N0RM LLC unit, and he is happy to let her satiate what she needs satiated so he can be out here working out what he needs to work out. That is one of the best benefits of the unit. It allows them to see to their individual needs more completely.

The dank garage smells of rubber and chemical solvents, gasoline and motor oil. Derek loves it, this smell of virility, which reaches him even through the full-face respirator with replaceable filters on both sides.

He is geared up.

He likes this part.

He wears 3M folding earmuffs for soundproofing, ear plugs beneath those, heavy duty gloves, and a PVC-coated rubber apron. He looks like a meth cook ready to break bad.

Last week at an estate auction he got a rusted-to-shit 1948 356, one of Porsche's first production automobiles. Hose in hand, he stands before the bubble coupe now. It is classic as hell, strong Connery-Bond vibes. It still runs, badly but consistently.

At his side is the Dustless Blasting DB500, a massive green-and-black compressor. Its silver belly holds water and recycled bottle glass. He loads the compressor with 40/70 grit recycled glass, which looks like sand until you spread it in your palm, and the ambers and greens twinkle to life.

The hose is the most powerful he has ever held, firing at 120 pounds per square inch. He will use it to blast off the rust, Bondo, primer, and old paint, bringing the car back to fresh steel.

He lies flat on his back, bracing himself before initiating the dead-man trigger. The hose flexes and fills behind him, python-like, and when the blast comes, the force nearly slides him across the oil-slick floor. Shoving his boots against the concrete, he holds on and directs the jet of glass-flecked water at the side of the Porsche. His entire torso is engaged, a massive upper-body workout. It's like an auto machine gun emitting a constant stream of lead.

In stages he acclimates to the roar of the compressor. As he inchworms himself along the floor, stripping the coats off the steel body, the jet engine rumble lulls him into complacency.

He does not notice the masculine form walking across his front lawn at a leisurely pace.

Nor does he notice when it enters the garage.

Derek is busy straining and flexing and aiming and sweating.

Bare feet approach. A shadow falls across him, but he cannot notice, not through the respirator.

He doesn't even sense the tug on the hose, just enough to whip the nozzle across his thigh.

The bite of crushed glass awakens him, shooting through the apron, his jeans, his flesh, drilling neatly down clear to the bone of the femur. At first he feels only a dreadful pressure.

He releases the nozzle, the dead-man switch shutting off the unit.

And then comes the blood, gushing from the gunshot-neat hole. If he has nicked his femoral artery, he is dead.

It is very, very close.

He is forgetting to breathe. He cannot see, the respirator fogged up. He shoves at the straps but cannot get the device off his head. Rolling onto his back, he feels the first premonition of discomfort, and then pain comes on, freight-train hard, the damaged limb screaming.

Writhing in pain, he catches a glimpse of something near his head. A shadow? A form? A man? It is hard to see, given the static dotting his visual field.

There is not much time. He must reach his phone. He must get help.

The form steps calmly around his head.

The door to the coupe opens and closes.

Derek's vision gets worse, everything swimming, choked with snow. He struggles to stay conscious.

The Porsche backs out of the garage, nearly crushing Derek's head.

As it drives off, he is still grappling beneath his apron for his cell phone.

Chapter 33

Mr. Man does not come home that night.

Rebecca and Mark have no idea what to do.

Maybe he is gathering solutions for them, as when he returned with the purloined bunny. Maybe he is berserking through the neighborhood, leaving traces of the family DNA at crime scenes. Maybe he is gone for good. What then?

Do they call the police? And say *what* precisely?

There is no protocol for this, no road map.

The passage of time feels like torture. Seconds tick by. Rebecca does not know what to do with her body, how to get comfortable, how to get off the treadmill of her looping thoughts.

She and Mark let Maddy sleep between them for the first time in years, the nigh-night routine thrown wildly out of whack. Maddy sprawls jumping-jack wide, shoving them to the edges of the king-size bed.

When Rebecca manages to doze off, she dreams that she cannot fall asleep, which makes it all the more exhausting when she jerks awake after five minutes of purgatory.

Mark is sleeping hard but keeps his arm stretched across the mattress to hold her wrist, as he does when she needs him and he needs her. His hand clenches softly, twitching as he battles night demons. His touch is the only thing that gets her through the night hours.

She awakens from another burst of not-quite sleep.

At last there is fragile light at the windows. The morning is quiet.

No clank of pans, no smell of fresh-roast coffee, no sounds of another body moving in the house.

Maddy is still out, radiator hot beneath the sheets. Mark's hand is sweaty on Rebecca's wrist. The morning sun, tinged a calming amber through the shades, blankets her face. Birdsong reaches her, warbles and chirps.

For a time, Rebecca lies perfectly still, listening to the sound of the natural world and her family breathing.

What is this sensation she feels?

Relief?

Freedom?

Maybe, she hopes, it will all prove to be a dream. Maybe she will walk down the hall, and the beautiful blue nursery will be empty as it was before, cribless and humanly sad in a manner she is designed to contend with, however painful it may be. Maybe there will be no rectangular prism, and she and Mark will be able to resume their life together with all its pain, challenges, and human triumphs.

She manages to slip out of bed without awakening Mark or Maddy.

Holding her breath, she walks down the hall, light on her feet. She peers around the corner.

The prism is still there, bulky and immovable.

The lid is up.

It is empty.

Mr. Man is not waiting in the kitchen.

"Bao-Bao" waits patiently in his cage for a morning carrot, which she delivers through the wire grid.

She makes her own coffee. The simple act of measuring and grinding the beans, inserting the filter, adding the water fills her with surprising contentedness.

More and more, it seems to Rebecca that humanity has reached the end of an era, that more and more of our work is being done for us, that we can outsource and push-button and delegate our tasks and needs until everything exists outside of us. Until we are hollow.

With satisfaction, she listens to the coffee maker burble and brew. It seems so old-fashioned, so obviously pleasing to do something herself.

When the pot is ready, she fills a mug decorated with Maddy's first-grade school portrait, in which she is smiling as if she never learned how to smile, teeth bared like an adorable and slightly confused chimpanzee.

Still in her jammies, Rebecca carries her coffee outside. The morning chill seeps through the fabric, bracing and invigorating. She's forgotten how much she cherishes this time, when the family is asleep and she is alone to greet the new day.

Breeze and birdsong open her to optimism. Perhaps it all has been just a misunderstanding with Mr. Man, as Luca suggested. Mixed signals about Bao-Bao and a footprint left when Mr. Man went to find her necklace for her. N0RM LLC is a legitimate corporation after all, its founder a Sun Valley regular. That means it has legal departments and quality control protocols, actuarial science, and liability concerns. They aren't going to release deadly product into the world. Can't self-protective capitalism confer some—any—measure of trust?

Her mighty pine thrusts three stories high, stoic against the wind. As she nears, she lets her gaze climb north.

The early sunlight illuminates it through and through, and she notices what she has not noticed before, that half of her tree, the west fork, is dying. The branches shed mosaic tiles of bark, and the needles look gray and dry. The west fork is a tree unto itself, heavy, powerful, thick, and the site of its dwindling fills her with dread.

Warming her hands around her mug, she thinks about everything her tree has seen. She'd read somewhere that pines can live over five hundred years.

A hand comes down on her shoulder, and she starts, coffee spilling over the lip, singeing her knuckles. Whipping around, she sees Mark.

"You didn't hear me?" he asks. "I called your name."

He is dressed for work.

She tents her fingers over the top of the mug so she can shake her other hand. "Sorry. Lost in thought."

"Derek called," Mark says. "He needs to see me immediately."

"You can tell Derek—"

"Not like that," Mark says. "He's at the hospital. He was nearly killed last night."

It sweeps through her now, a black wave of despair.

This nightmare, it seems, has not ended.

It is only beginning.

Chapter 34

Derek is spiderweb ensnared in the hospital bed, wrapped in cords and bandages and lines. From what Mark can gather at first glance, Derek is plugged into a heart monitor, a pulse oximeter, a blood pressure cuff, two IVs, and drainage tubing. Or they are plugged into him. It's hard to tell which way the system flows; he looks like a cyberhuman, like Luke Skywalker in the bacta tank. Derek's eyes are groggy from drugs, his lids pouched. His normally coifed hair is matted, his face crusty from sleep, and he is too drugged and traumatized to remember to ask Mark about strep throat.

Mark has never seen him less than shiny. In fact, with the Teflon exterior scraped off, he looks profoundly mortal.

He continues on in a rasp, his vocals still shot from the intubation. "Thought I was gonna die. Sparkly glow, tunnel of light, all that."

Mark draws close to the bed. "You didn't see who yanked the hose?"

Derek's head rolls back and forth on the pillow, a weary no. "Random act of violence. You know how this city's getting."

Mark's insides are boiling with suspicion, paranoia, and fear, but he contains himself. "Where's Alexa?"

Derek takes a long blink. He looks like a lost little boy. "She came last night. Had to get home. To sleep, you know. Needs to stay strong with me in here."

But he cannot hide his loneliness, the terrible vulnerability writ large across his face.

"I'm sorry," Mark says, because he cannot think of anything else to say. And he realizes that it is more than a knee-jerk response, that he actually means it.

"Missed my femoral artery by this much." Derek lifts a trembling hand and measures a few millimeters between his thumb and a forefinger made bulbous by the pulse ox. "Nerve damage, they said." His words slightly blurry. "Vascular injury needs another surgery."

"But you're gonna be okay?"

"Won't be getting back to kickboxing anytime soon."

"How long are you out?"

"Two, three weeks," Derek says. "'S why I asked you here."

Mark looks at him, puzzled.

"I know we've had our differences." Derek's forehead is tight with concentration, the way Maddy's gets sometimes. It is taking all his focus to speak. "And I never realized how much I can count on you. Not until I was lying here thinking about who needs to take the reins on product operations while I'm out."

Mark knows that Derek is right, that he is the best choice to get the company back on track, but he cannot believe that he is hearing it from Derek.

Derek makes a weird noise. It takes a moment for Mark to identify it as a whimper.

Derek's eyes get glassy. He is crying. The sight of it, for some reason, is awful. His face jerks unattractively. He looks so different from his impeccably groomed self.

Something gnaws at Mark's chest. Pity? Empathy? Whatever it is, it works like acid on his resentment, dissolving it into a puddle of dismay.

"Alexa only stayed twenty minutes," Derek says, slurring with tears and morphine. "How long would Rebecca have stayed if it was you? Or you for her?"

Mark knows in this moment that lying would not be merciful. So he tells the truth. "All night," he says. "All the way through."

Derek closes his eyes, tears clinging to the gunk on his lashes. He nods once, a dip of the chin, only down. He knew the answer already. "Can you run things while I'm out?"

Mark says, "If you trust me to."

"I do. Thank you, Mark. Thank you." A wobbly hand rises, trailing lines and cords.

Mark takes it. It isn't a handshake. More like they hold hands for a moment, the touch oddly intimate.

He looks down at Derek's tear-glassy eyes, and something passes between them.

"'M sorry," Derek says. ". . . Sorry."

His head sags to the side as he drifts off.

Chapter 35

Mr. Man is fully charged.

That is good.

He has lots to handle still.

He has been busy.

It is hard to follow someone, to figure out their schedule, to wait for the perfect opening.

As long as he stays in the car, he can blend in. He changed the license plates already and gave the Porsche a quick black coat using spray paint he stole from an automotive store late last night.

Parked outside the residence, he waits and watches for his target.

He needs the right opening, the right angle, and a lack of witnesses.

It will be challenging.

But that is okay.

Mr. Man is up for a challenge.

And once he takes care of this, he will move on to the thing that he must take care of.

The Higgins family still needs so much more of his help.

Chapter 36

Rebecca and Maddy arrive at school early so Rebecca can work kiss-and-ride. Greeting kids, hauling backpacks out of trunks, dealing with rich parents who don't heed the simple traffic rules, who don't bother to get off their cell phones, who treat the volunteers like hired help.

Gray clouds pile up atop one another, threatening rain, which seems unseasonable in Los Angeles, no matter the season. Nerves jangle inside Rebecca as she breathes the wet air and waits for Mark's call from the hospital.

It finally comes in, of course, at peak drop-off time. She cannot stop herself from answering, even as cars pile up and horns bleat. Her attention is split between the call and a tricky trunk latch.

"Someone stole one of his antique Porsches and injured him bad," Mark is saying. "But he doesn't know who."

She turns, shielding the phone from the wind. "We know who, don't we?"

A black silence stretches out. She pictures Mark trying to come up with a response.

She rescues him, asking, "You going home?"

"Office. Derek asked me to take over while he's in the hospital."

"*Really*? That's . . ."

"Incredible? Unlikely? I know. Any sign of Mr. Man, just leave the house and I'll come right away to handle it. I can leave whenever, now that, you know, I'm the new jefe."

She loves hearing the playful lilt back in his voice. How long he's been waiting for a shot of confidence, to have his competence pay dividends.

A horn blares at her. "Wrong backpack!" A young father in a Mercedes screams at her, Bluetooth earpiece screwed into his head. "Hey, lady, *wrong backpack!*"

A general rule Rebecca has learned: The rudeness of a parent is proportional to the price of his vehicle. She returns the *Dora the Explorer* backpack to the trunk, removes *The Avengers*.

The fourth grader grabs it from her without a word of thanks, shoulders it, and runs off.

The Mercedes screeches away and—of course—Sheila's Jaguar pulls up next.

"Congrats, jefe, but I gotta go," Rebecca whispers and hangs up.

Though it is barely seven o'clock in the morning, Sheila is made up for the red carpet. Augmented lips, plumped and painted a metallic rose gold, match her sleek manicure. Her hair looks like it was professionally blown out already, likely from a residential hairdresser since no reasonable salon is open at this hour. Her silk camisole is full Saks Fifth Avenue, and she is braless, her nipples hard. In the passenger seat sits the wide-mouthed brunette from the disastrous encounter at Sheila's house, equally glammed up, chicken-pecking at her phone with an index finger bent back to protect the gel nail. Her head is tilted down, and Rebecca feels a stab of schadenfreude at an intimation of a double chin.

Sheila's voice is loud enough to be heard over the traffic; she is ordering someone to make her and "the girls" a brunch reservation at Ivy at the Shore.

Her gaze sweeps right across Rebecca, who stands there in her sweats and Monterey Bay Aquarium sweatshirt, waiting for the Jaguar's trunk to be popped. She might as well be a street sign, a mailbox, a fire hydrant.

As Sydney clambers out, Sheila says, "Give Mommy a kiss."

Sydney obeys dutifully.

Sheila's eyes snag on Rebecca. And once again move right past. Still speaking into her dashboard, Sheila drives away.

Rebecca helps Sydney into her backpack, a leather-strapped Herschel that seems far too fancy for an eight-year-old.

"Thanks, Mrs. Higgins."

"You're welcome, Sydney."

"You gonna be at student showcase night tonight?"

"I sure will."

"Mom says she's not sure she can make it."

"I hope she does."

"Me too," Sydney says and scurries off.

Rebecca waves the next car forward to her orange cone. Vehicles are backed up all the way past the light, *Tetris*-ing their way through Westside congestion. Patrick is gesticulating angrily with the handheld stop sign. Ever since he was assigned traffic oversight, he has gone mad with power.

A Range Rover veers up too fast, front tire grinding the curb, and Rebecca takes a hop back. A dad wearing wraparound sunglasses gives her a flick of his hand to open the rear door and help his two sons out.

The boys spill free and sprint toward the playground, and the next car lurches forward.

After her shift, Rebecca needs to hit the grocery store, fill the fridge, clean not-Bao-Bao's cage, prepare hummus and veggie plates for student showcase night, pick up Maddy, oversee homework, and be back at the school early for setup before the influx of arriving parents.

It will be a long day, but she will manage.

Unless, of course, Mr. Man shows up.

Chapter 37

The day is wall-to-wall, but even as Rebecca rushes around, the threat of Mr. Man's reemergence lingers at the base of her brain, an itch she can't scratch.

She feeds Maddy at home quickly, microwave burritos from TJ's, and shoves a few carrots at not-Bao-Bao.

When at last they arrive at student showcase night, it takes Rebecca several trips to unload the hummus platters from car to classroom. Though it is still the backend of twilight, the sky has gone midnight dark beneath the blanket of clouds, and the air feels electric, portentous. Some of the other parents are standing around gossiping, and resentment nips at Rebecca's heels as she rushes back and forth to the parking lot.

An oft-cited quotation from her overbearing mother sails into her head: *Resentment is like drinking poison and waiting for the other person to die.* Someone important said it, Saint Augustine or Nelson Mandela. Delivered through her mother, a woman who allows zero oxygen for communication disruptive to her worldview, the words always coasted to Rebecca's ears on fumes of hypocrisy.

And yet, fumbling to maintain her grip on the third tray, she reclaims them now. Why the hell is she so useless at speaking up for herself? Is she really content to play victim for the rest of her life?

As she buzzes around the classroom, pulling saran wrap off the hummus, she overhears Girl Dylan's mother sniping that the platters look premade.

Rebecca clears her throat, musters ancient courage, says, "Actually I put them together myself today. From scratch."

Girl Dylan's mother colors, her face tensing. "I'm sorry. I didn't mean to imply . . ." She catches herself because, of course, she did mean to imply. Then something magical happens. She rests a hand on Rebecca's forearm. "Thank you," she says. "I always notice how much you do."

Rebecca smiles back and turns away quickly, not wanting anyone to see her welling up. She is such a crybaby. And yet a burst of adrenaline hums through her, accompanied with a kind of long-forgotten optimism that feels like a return to herself.

Maddy rushes up to take her by the hand. "Mommy, I haveta show you my work!" She propels Rebecca over to a classroom wall covered with drawings and craft projects. Giant construction paper letters declaim: **These Are a Few of My Favorite Things!**

Rebecca scans the stapled offerings, searching out Maddy's distinctive signature among the panoply of offerings.

Next to an oft-practiced sketch of a stegosaurus, there's a crayon drawing of Maddy and Rebecca in front of a mirror. *One of my favorate things is when Mommy brushs my hair!*

She finds another: *I love it when Daddy drivs me to school and dos his funny voice!*

Warmth spills through her. Seeing how her countless quotidian efforts have landed, how many bits and pieces of her and Mark's care have roosted inside their girl, sets Rebecca abuzz. It is like drifting through a dream.

Anuther favorate thing is my ni-nite routine with Mommy when we give the stuffties sleep-tite hugs!

One of my favorate things is brekfast when its just me and my parents.

I love doing my nitetime afurmations with Mommy and Daddy becuase they teach me to be my best selv.

"Her spelling's coming along," a voice beside her says. "Almost grade level. It's *so* good she's starting to catch up."

Rebecca turns to see Sheila standing beside her, breathing white wine, cheeks flushed, her eyes crinkled with artificial goodwill.

Rebecca feels the scalpel thrust, starts to recoil. But then a pulse of wickedness flicks up to the surface. "Sheila," she replies, "how nice you could make it."

Even through expertly administered Botox, Sheila's eyes flare slightly. She swallows visibly and steps away, loose on her feet. Rebecca wonders how many glasses of wine she has consumed since brunch.

Then she sees Maddy beelining for her from the brownie platter, chocolate smears around her mouth. Crouching, she catches Maddy in a hug, lets her brownie-grubby hands and face bury themselves in her sensible sweater. She loves it, loves the mess, loves having her daughter tangle herself up in her and for once not giving a shit what anyone else might think of anything.

"I'm so proud of you, Maddysaurus," Rebecca breathes into her ear.

"You like my pictures?"

"Love them. Wanna know what *my* favorite thing is?"

Maddy smiles big, points at the dead center of her own chest.

"That's right."

Maddy's tiny fingers find her pendant and then Rebecca's, and Rebecca helps her piece them together to form a whole heart. That is how she is starting to feel for the first time in a long time. Whole.

When she rises again, she notices that Sheila has left.

Chapter 38

The parking lot is so crammed that navigating to freedom is like leaving a packed concert at the Hollywood Bowl. Creeping along in the minivan, Rebecca has Disney on Sirius. Maddy is singing along to "Let It Go" at the top of her lungs and making the stegosaurus lunch box, which has been moldering beneath the back seat since this afternoon, dance along. A light rain spits at the windshield, promising worse to come.

At last they are out onto the street, Patrick waving them along vigorously with the stop sign he seems to have on his person at all times, like a security blanket. Even threading through lesser-known residential roads, it takes a while for Rebecca to escape the clutches of congestion, every block providing more breathing room until they finally reach a pace suited to an automobile.

The streets suddenly are empty. Mist-shrouded treetops swoop by overhead. The windshield wipers give an unsettling squeak, smudging moisture back and forth ineffectively. She signals dutifully, begins a cautious turn onto the next street.

Even over the radio, she hears it.

The sound of car tires screeching, a prolonged skid.

And then the gut-dropping crunch of colliding metal.

As she sweeps through the turn, wipers beating manically, she makes out a crumpled red Jaguar SUV launched brutally across a tiny strip of front lawn and through the side of a house. Way ahead, taillights glower like demon eyes as the hit-and-run driver snakes across the next intersection and disappears into the gloom.

"Mommy, what is it?" Maddy is practically standing up off her car seat, the belt straining across her chest. "What happened?"

Rebecca pulls over and leaps out. "Stay here, honey. Just—stay here."

The rain has intensified, soaking through her hair instantly, chilling her scalp, sluicing across her face. She is already dialing 911, speaking to the operator as she approaches, rattling off the street and intersection.

No one is home in the breached house, or at least the lights are off. The Jag is tangled up in the wall, the rear third smashed right through into the family room.

All the SUV's windows have shattered, the deployed driver airbag beating against the dashboard with the wind. A form, Sheila's form, is tipped forward toward the steering wheel, face buried in the saggy pillow of high-strength nylon.

Motionless.

"Someone's hurt here," Rebecca says into the phone. "Hurt bad."

From the back seat, a voice cries out. No words, just a drawn-out cry of terror.

Sydney.

Ashen, shaken, but intact.

"I gotta go," Rebecca tells the operator. "Get someone here now."

Sydney spots Rebecca and begins to wail.

Rebecca moves to the rear window, reaching through the pebbled maw. "It's okay, honey. I'm here. You're safe. I got you now."

Sydney stares at her, shell shocked. She looks okay—no bruising, no cuts. The side curtain airbag seems to have caught her; it, too, lulls in the wind that is blowing straight through the vehicle. The door is hammered shut so Rebecca leans through the shattered window, unlocks her seat belt, and guides her out.

Sydney clings to her neck and helps shove herself free. It takes some doing.

Rebecca runs her back to the minivan, clicking to slide the door open. Maddy waits, wide eyed and breathing hard.

"Sydney, wait here with Maddy. I'm gonna check on your mom."

Sydney's nod is a series of jerks.

Rebecca helps her in, closes the door, runs back to the Jag.

Sheila is still tilted forward, head embedded in the deflated air bag. Even over the acrid chemical smell from the airbag propellant, Rebecca can smell a tinge of white wine.

Steeling herself, she reaches a hand toward Sheila's neck, trying for a pulse.

Before she can make contact, there comes a sharp gurgle. Sheila's body twitches and leans stiffly back in the driver's seat.

Her face seems to be gone. What remains is a red mask.

A forehead laceration bleeds freely, sheeting blood across her face. The nose is badly broken, smeared to the side and torn wide open down the front to expose the nasal cavity. One eye is swollen shut. The other stabs out of the morass, focusing on Rebecca. Swollen lips part. A hiss issues forth. A bubble of crimson-laced saliva forms at the mouth and then pops.

Rebecca takes her hand before realizing that the fingers are jangled inorganically, broken at the knuckles. "It's okay," she whispers hoarsely.

"Sydney," the face hisses.

"I have her. She's okay. She's not hurt. I have her. I have her."

Mercifully, Rebecca hears sirens.

Sheila's neck buckles, head lolling. Rebecca takes it, eases it back onto the headrest, her palms sticky against the abraded flesh. "Just hang on. Help is coming."

"Take . . . Sydney . . . home . . ."

"I will. As soon as the paramedics check her, I'll get her safely home. I promise."

The siren scream peaks, the broken glass all around them dancing with reflected reds and blues.

"Don't worry. Just breathe. You're gonna be okay."

Footsteps approaching. "Ma'am, stand clear. Stand clear, please, and let us do our job."

Rebecca obeys. "There's a child, too, who was in the car when it was hit."

"Where is she?"

"In my van. In my minivan."

Two of the paramedics are working on Sheila. A third hustles to the minivan, and Rebecca follows to open the door.

Hugging herself across the stomach, she stands in the rain. She pictures Mr. Man in the kitchen the other morning, quietly listening when she told her husband and daughter how much she'd like to sue Sheila right in the face.

Chapter 39

It is nearly eleven o'clock by the time Rebecca drives Sydney home. Maddy stays at Sydney's side, holding hands as the three of them make their way up the walkway, carved through lush landscaping. Unseen lighting bleaches the air with a trio of flashes, waves of thunder rumbling at them on a few seconds' delay. They are soaked through and through, teeth chattering.

Rebecca has updated Mark at intervals, and he is already heading home to wait for them. The thought is an immense comfort.

They continue toward the expansive house. Because Rebecca called ahead, the butler and nanny are waiting in the foyer, the architectural front door already open beneath the modern portico.

As they near, Sydney reaches for Rebecca's hand. She stands there between Maddy and Rebecca.

"Where is . . ." Rebecca hesitates, trying to remember the dad's name. "Her father?"

"In New York on business," the butler says.

The nanny gestures for Sydney to come in. Sydney does not let go of Rebecca's and Maddy's hands.

"Come," the nanny says brusquely, with a heavy accent. "Bath time."

"She's been through a lot," Rebecca said.

The nanny makes a clucking noise, as if shooing a dog, as she steps forward and tugs Sydney free.

The giant glass door closes, and Sydney is marched back toward one of the colossal hallways.

Rebecca and Maddy stand helplessly on the wide concrete porch, watching her recede. Before Sydney disappears from view, she casts a glance back over her shoulder.

Her chin quivers.

And she is gone.

"She gonna be okay, Mommy?"

Rebecca takes Maddy's hand, and they hustle back to the van, ducking against the downpour. "She'll have to be, honey."

They climb into the minivan, and Rebecca turns over the engine, blasts the heat.

But she does not drive away. Instead she sits there, hands on the steering wheel. The rain has hardened her skin to rubber, but she feels oddly renewed, washed clean.

"What, Mommy?"

Rebecca draws in a deep breath. "You were right," she says. "About Bao-Bao."

Maddy's head is drawn back, nearly invisible blond eyebrows lifted. "Bao-Bao isn't Bao-Bao?"

"No."

"What happened to Bao-Bao?"

"Mr. Man thought he was food."

Maddy's lips form a plump *O*. "So he ate him?"

"No. But he . . . killed him to cook him."

Maddy studies her intently in the rearview mirror. "But you didn't let him cook Bao-Bao."

"No."

"Why did he think Bao-Bao was food?"

"It was a misunderstanding."

"Like the stinky cheese."

"Yes. Like the stinky cheese."

"But you told me Bao-Bao was Bao-Bao."

"I lied," Rebecca says. "I lied to you. And I'm sorry."

"But we don't lie."

"I know, honey. We're not supposed to lie."

"So why did you?"

"I didn't want you to feel bad. And I felt . . . guilty, I guess. Responsible."

"For what Mr. Man did?"

"For wanting to have a Mr. Man to begin with." The answers are right there for Rebecca, though she has not considered them before. "When it should have been just you, me, and Daddy."

Maddy's expression is exemplarily thoughtful, a face carved by Rodin. "It's okay, Mommy. It wasn't your fault. And it wasn't Mr. Man's fault."

"Why . . ." Rebecca's voice wobbles, and she pauses to swallow. "Why wasn't it his fault?"

"He didn't know better. Neither did you."

"Thank you, honey." Rebecca drops the gear shift into Drive and forges into the battering rain. "But now I do."

Chapter 40

The minivan creeps through the squall, windshield wipers thrashing.

Los Angeles is ill prepared for a storm. Trees topple, hillsides avalanche, and accumulated oil and grease form a film across the roads, derailing SoCal drivers. Power lines are down, sparking in the streets. Mailboxes have been upended, spat from the soft earth. The way is choked with tow trucks ambling to their next appointments, with cars that have drifted up onto sidewalks, with folks hauling sandbags to form bulwarks at curbs or garage door seams.

Maddy is half asleep in her car seat, jaw slack, head cast back, her throat bowing outward. Rebecca proceeds cautiously, but the minivan still threatens to hydroplane at every turn.

At last she eases onto their street, crawling past Jackson's dark house toward their driveway.

A blast hurtles from the heavens, bright enough to scorch her pupils. Only when she blinks can she see what it is in the afterimpression scorched onto the inside of her eyelids—a massive lightning bolt zigzagging down to impale the giant pine tree. It sends out a firework cascade of sparks.

She slams the brake pedal, hard enough to skid a few feet and send Maddy's head lurching forward.

For an instant, the pine is engulfed in flame from the inside, a lava seam running beneath the bark. There comes a fearsome groan and a top-heavy shift of mass in the darkness above.

The dead fork of the tree gives way, whipping past the house, a near miss, to crash into the driveway ten feet in front of the hood of the minivan. The other half of the tree is still enflamed, crackling with destruction. Rebecca and Maddy watch with something like reverence as it sloughs its skin, much of its bulk crumbling to the lawn and across the neighboring hedge, sizzling in the rain.

Awestruck, Rebecca drifts out of the minivan to stand in the puddled street. She hears the door pop open behind her, and then Maddy is at her side, and they stand, and they stare.

The dry, shedding parts of the pine lie in smoldering heaps, but the living shaft, the part that is green and strong and bleeding sap, still stands tall, shed of its dead weight.

It is pointing straight up like a flagpole, like a rifle, like a Gothic spire aimed at the star-beaded darkness overhead.

Thunder rushes them, vibrating straight through their bones. Maddy gives a yelp and tucks behind Rebecca.

Another jag of lightning blasts down a few blocks away, illuminating the front of the house, and there is a masculine figure on their porch, and it is not Mr. Man, it is Mark, and in a sudden burst of mom-strength Rebecca hoists Maddy up, slinging her across one hip as she did when Maddy was a toddler, and she blazes through the parasitical wreckage, and the rain snipes down the floating embers, and then she is in Mark's arms, she and Maddy are in Mark's arms, a huddle of three on the porch, and Mark is holding them, holding them both, and he kisses Rebecca's head and says, "It's okay now, you're home," and they stagger half dead into the quiet of the house.

Chapter 41

It is less a sleep than an ego death, an exhausting trance of nonbeing. Hours later, Rebecca stirs in the same position she fell onto the bed—flat on her stomach, face mashed half on the pillow. Her mouth is dry, sour with sleep.

It is still pouring out, rain drumming the roof, thunder roaring like a revved engine, the world tearing itself apart in its ancient dance.

Maddy is passed out beside her, but Mark is not there on his side of the bed.

He stands facing the door, muscles tensed, on high alert.

Rebecca shoves herself up. "What?" she whispers hoarsely.

Mark holds two fingers out to his side, turns slowly. "Hear that?" he whispers back.

A faint sound comes audible over the storm.

Clink clink. Clink clink.

It originates from somewhere down the hall.

Somewhere near the nursery.

She finds her feet, pulls on a sweatshirt, takes her place at Mark's side.

Clink clink. Clink clink.

They look back at Maddy, a final check before leaving the safety of the bedroom.

The sound comes even louder off the hard surfaces of the hall.

Clink clink. Clink clink.

They inch down the corridor, eyes on the nursery door.

It is open.

Did they leave it open? She cannot remember.

Clink clink. Clink clink.

The noise is oddly even, perfectly spaced like Mr. Man's fingers and toes.

They draw closer, the sound of their progress muted by the hammering of rain on the shingles. It is like being inside a kettledrum. Lightning flashes, throwing the framed photographs on the wall into sudden bright relief—coconut drinks on their Kauai honeymoon, Maddy's kindergarten portrait, a selfie of them crammed three across on that bunny slope ski lift at Big Bear.

Clink clink. Clink clink.

The nursery is now just a few strides away.

But Mark halts by the laundry-room cubby. The door is closed.

When he opens it, the *clink clink* grows louder yet.

Bleach sits atop the washing machine. Laundry thumps inside the dryer. Who is washing anything at this hour?

Mark's knee cracks as he squats before the dryer. He reaches for the handle. Hesitates. Tugs it open.

A tumble of clothes inside.

A T-shirt from Costco. A pair of Mark's 501s.

Clink clink. Clink clink.

Like something left in a pocket of the jeans has come loose.

As the dryer slows, the thing inside rattles loudly to a stop.

Rebecca splits her focus between the dryer, the nursery door just ahead, and the dark hall beyond.

Mark reaches inside. His hand disappears to the wrist in fabric, roots around.

It emerges.

His shoulders ripple as they tighten. He gives something like a gasp.

Rebecca's heart is thundering to match the storm. She jerks her gaze to check the hall once more and then leans to peer over his shoulder.

A silver key, the head bulging tumorlike to the right.

But that isn't what snares her breath in her throat. It's the leather fob the key is attached to, sporting a metal crest with the Porsche insignia.

Mark sets down the key on top of the dryer. He stands slowly.

The rise and fall of his chest beneath his T-shirt, a match for the one in the dryer, is pronounced.

They brace themselves. Ease forward to the nursery.

Shadows from the fallen tree limbs wag jerkily against baby blue walls.

The room and prism are empty.

Rebecca's lungs burn with anticipation. She remembers to exhale.

Back into the hall.

A creak issues from the kitchen.

Mark moves more swiftly now, and she skips once to keep pace. She does not want to be out of his reach.

They come through the brief foyer and into the kitchen, and there Mr. Man is, standing before the open bunny cage, holding not-Bao-Bao in his arms.

The fallen fork of the tree twists outside the bay windows, a tentacle heaved up from the deep. A strobe of lightning flickers across Mr. Man's bland-featured mask, patterning the wall behind him with fans of needles.

Rebecca's words come as a hot hiss: "What did you do?"

Mr. Man strokes the rabbit. "Nothing you did not want me to take care of."

"That's not true," Mark says. "That's not true at all."

"You have not consulted yourselves," Mr. Man says, "deeply enough."

His hand tightens on the rabbit's scruff, tugging it upward. Rebecca braces herself for a snap or a crunch, but none comes.

"I want this to end," Rebecca says. "We want this to end."

"Listen," Mark says, trying for calm and steady, "we don't want this to turn violent. Let's just get you back in the prism."

Mr. Man stares at them with that blank face, those dead eyes. Beyond the bay windows, the branches of the fallen tree shudder in the breeze, a procession of the dead. Lightning shocks the night again, throwing his shadow gothically across the cornflower blue of the Pottery Barn couch and the rest of the ridiculous furnishings. The stainless steel facade of the microwave flashes, as does the titanium business card on the desk, the card that started this all.

His mouth shapes a crescent. It is a smile, though it does not look like a smile. The mouth says, "But our work is not done. I have not taken care of your mother yet."

Ice water moves through Rebecca's veins. She tries to take a breath but cannot. What else is on Mr. Man's checklist? On *her* checklist?

"Mommy? Daddy?"

"Go back to your room, Maddy," Mark says. "Right now."

But Maddy does not listen. Holding Mr. Fox by the ears, she stands and observes Mr. Man.

"You killed Bao-Bao," she says.

Mr. Man's head cocks as he regards her. "Yes. I did."

"You didn't understand what to do."

"No. I did not."

"You don't understand a lot," Maddy says. "That's okay. I sometimes don't either."

"We are trying," Mark says through clenched teeth, "to get Mr. Man back into his prism."

"He's not safe right now, honey," Rebecca says. "He's not safe anymore."

Maddy's calm gaze moves from them across to Mr. Man and then back to them again. She gives her one-shouldered shrug.

She walks over to the desk.

She picks up the titanium business card.

She brings it back to Rebecca and Mark.

It is shiny in her small hand.

It glints up at them.

It says: **YOU'RE IN CHARGE**.

At the sight of it, Rebecca's and Mark's last requests play like echoes in Rebecca's mind.

Maybe you should go back in.

I think we'd do well to take a break. Wouldn't you like to take a break too?

We'd like you to get back into the prism.

We don't want this to turn violent. Let's just get you back in the prism.

Everything phrased indirectly, elliptically, with equivocation.

Rebecca takes the hard-edged card. Stares down at the words. Feels something rising within her, something young and buried and firm of purpose.

Her eyes lift to laser into Mr. Man, and her voice takes on the timbre of a foreman on a job that allows no overtime. "Go to the nursery," she says. *"Now."*

Mr. Man remains still for a second too long.

And then he is walking toward them.

Rebecca braces, but Mr. Man walks right past her and Mark, heading toward the foyer.

They follow him up the hall to the nursery. Rebecca enters after him, Mark behind, holding Maddy's hand.

"Get in," Rebecca says.

Mr. Man approaches the bulky prism. Above the laser-etched **NORM LLC**, the sensor light glows green. The lid is propped up.

He rests his hands on the rim. Then turns to look back at her over his shoulder. His face is expressionless, but there is something about it that seems to be pleading.

Rebecca says it again: *"Get. In."*

Mr. Man climbs in.

"Close the lid."

Mr. Man blinks and then blinks again. His smooth hand reaches for an internal control and pulses, and then the lid lowers down slowly, slowly, wiping him from view.

His dark pupils are the last thing Rebecca sees before the prism seals.

"Do not come out of here," she tells the closed casket, "ever again."

She takes a step back and then another, until she is standing beside Mark and Maddy.

And then Mark walks over to the 240-volt charging point and rips the fat cord out of the wall.

The green sensor light flickers once and dies.

Chapter 42

Rebecca wakes up to the sound of Mark's voice. He is sitting on the love seat by the closet where he casts his jacket and his to-be-worn-again jeans with the belt still through the loops. He is dressed for work, sipping coffee, laptop open across his knees. Though it is early, he looks as awake as he has ever been. Maddy lies sprawled sideways by Rebecca, emitting a soft, whistling snore.

"As I told you, the unit has been unplugged," Mark is saying. "We want it picked up and disposed of immediately."

Luca's voice sounds more robotic than before. "As I mentioned, that is not in our contract."

"I don't care what's in our contract," Mark says. "Pick it up."

There is a coolness in his tone that Rebecca remembers from when they first met. That strength of conviction he had when he spoke about computer engineering, the Red Sox, when he got down on a knee and told her, *You are all that I want today and forever.*

"May I remind you that we have synced your personal information."

"You are to destroy that too," Mark says. "Any records of our family. Purge them from the databases. And memorialize on legal letterhead that you have done so and that our relationship is terminated."

"What makes you believe you have legal standing in this matter?"

"I don't have legal standing," Mark says. "I have *leverage*. I run an e-news content optimization service. I have arranged for damaging content about N0RM LLC to flood the internet in the event that this is not done. It is one click from happening."

There is a long silence, during which Rebecca imagines Luca, composed as ever, running countless calculations behind the mask of her face.

"Are you sure you want to go to war with us?"

"I'm sure that I do not," Mark says. "Nor do you with me. Whatever mess this causes will not be worth it for you or your pending IPO. Let's walk away clean, terminate the relationship. It's the best choice for both of us."

From the bed, Rebecca cannot see the screen, but she can see his unwavering gaze. His tie is cinched tight at his spread collar. He looks like a boss.

The silence stretches out and out.

And then Luca says, "I have availability for a six p.m. pickup today. Would that time be convenient?"

"Yes," Mark says and snaps down the laptop's lid.

For the first time, he notices Rebecca is awake.

He gives her his half smile. "What?"

"When'd you get so sexy?" she says, her back arching in a morning stretch.

Now the grin cracks wide. "Always have been," he says. "You just stopped noticing."

Chapter 43

Rebecca is driving Maddy to the beach when the cell phone rings, interrupting the Disney Channel. Caller ID shows an unfamiliar number. Swooping through the Palisades on Sunset Boulevard, she clicks to answer.

"Mrs. Higgins?"

"Yes?"

In the back seat, Maddy keeps Mr. Elephant dancing on her lap to "How Far I'll Go" from *Moana*, even though the music has stopped.

"My name is Jim. I'm the personal executive assistant to Sheila and Don Evans."

"How is she?"

"Mrs. Evans is stable. Thank you for your concern. She's undergoing reconstructive plastic surgery this afternoon. It'll be a long road back, but she'll be okay."

"I'm glad to hear that," Rebecca says and is happy to feel how deeply she means it.

"Mr. Evans wanted to thank you for the care you showed Sydney in the aftermath of the accident."

"Of course," Rebecca says.

"He wanted to send something over as a token of his appreciation."

"What might that be?"

"A new technology, still in beta phase. It's not yet to market, but because Mr. Evans invested heavily in the Series B, he has a plus-one he'd like to offer to you."

Rebecca laughs.

"I'm sorry, Mrs. Higgins. Is something amusing?"

"No," she says. "Please tell Mr. Evans he can save his plus-one for someone else." In the rearview she watches Mr. Elephant pirouette on Maddy's knee. "We're fine just as we are."

Chapter 44

They reach Zuma in Malibu, park in the overpriced lot, and hold hands across the stretch of cool sand. Maddy has no texture issues with sand, actually loves the feel of it between her bare toes.

As she splashes at the water edge and digs for sand crabs, Rebecca stares out across the endless ocean. Each swell seems like the earth taking a breath.

Since the sky has yet to shake off last night's storm, the beach is relatively empty, just a few solo walkers, an old lady with a labradoodle, and a clutch of not-to-be-deterred surfers floating in place, waiting on a good break.

Rebecca shoves her hands into the pockets of her hooded sweatshirt, makes a fist around the Porsche key from the dryer.

While Maddy is distracted, scaring seagulls into flight, Rebecca pulls the key free and hurls it into the ocean, fob and all.

It plunks into the water, the slate-gray surface closes around it, and it is as if the key never existed.

Rebecca shuts her eyes, tilts her face to the sun, and breathes the ocean air. All she can hear is the rush of the sea, the cawing of the gulls, and the sound of her daughter's laughter.

She never imagined that simple gratitude could feel so emancipating.

Chapter 45

Delivery Joe is back on their porch. Same hipster beard, same gauge earrings, different knit cap. The prism rests atop the futuristic dolly at his side, and the sleek, unmarked van waits at the curb.

Both front doors have been laid open to accommodate the prism's removal, and Mark hastens to close them now.

"Didn't work out, huh?" Delivery Joe says.

"Nope," Mark says. "Wasn't for us."

Maddy shuffles through the foyer, hugging not-Bao-Bao to her stomach, his front legs sticking straight out above her arms.

Delivery Joe produces an electronic pad from somewhere on the dolly and holds it out in his gloved hands. "Confirming the return." His breath carries a whiff of nicotine gum.

Rebecca takes the stylus and signs her name.

With a whir, the dolly revs into motion, its wheels rotating like tank tread to convey its load down the stairs. Mark and Rebecca stand in the doorway and watch it roll across the gouged-up lawn. A tree crew was here all day, chainsawing the wreckage of the tree and hauling it off.

The remaining pine looks strong yet vulnerable, fresh pulp exposed at the split.

Delivery Joe lays open the van's rear door, and then the dolly elevates on robot-dog legs, slides the prism inside, and climbs in around it, the effect like a spider disappearing into a tiny hole.

Mark and Rebecca stay until the van pulls out, until it drives up the street, until it turns the corner and disappears.

Chapter 46

For the first time in a long time, Mark and Rebecca take Maddy's nigh-night routine at a luxurious pace. It feels like when she was a newborn, when they were doing this for the first time.

Rebecca sings terribly to Maddy in the bath, scrunching the sponge on top of her head while Mark sits on the toilet and pretends to brush his teeth with the toilet scrubber. Maddy's belly laughs ring off the tile. Soap and shampoo, dry and lotion, Mark singing into the bottle of detangler, getting the words to "Let It Go" ridiculously incorrect. When Rebecca brushes Maddy's long, loose curls, Maddy leans back against her, still warm-wet in her crocodile bath wrap. Teeth are up next, Mark brushing next to her, foaming rabidly at the mouth long enough to make sure Maddy does her two minutes. Then it's time to pee and choose a nightgown—Tiana from *The Princess and the Frog*.

It is time to give goodnight kisses to "Bao-Bao."

They march into the kitchen together, and Maddy steers him gently out of the crate.

"Do you . . . Do you still want to keep him?" Rebecca asks.

Maddy nods furiously.

"What should we call him?" Mark says.

"Not Bao-Bao."

Rebecca seeks clarification. "Not-Bao-Bao? As a name? Or not Bao-Bao?"

"Not Bao-Bao."

Mark says, "Mr. Bunny?"

"I already *have* a Mr. Bunny," Maddy says, indignant.

"What then?"

Maddy screws her mouth to the side. "Bunnysaurus," she says. "Cuz he bit me."

"Bunnysaurus it is."

Goodnight kisses for Bunnysaurus are slightly tentative.

Then it's back to Maddy's bedroom for *sleep tight* hugs for the stuffties. Mark fluffs the pillows and tucks the blankets to Maddy's chin, inexplicably narrating everything with a brusque French accent.

Rebecca intones the long-suffering mother's refrain— "Don't wind her up"—but Maddy's giggles are contagious, and they all crack up, and they don't get settled down until halfway through *Horton. Good Night, Gorilla* and *Goodnight*

Moon go off without a hitch, and then Mark administers sleep-inducing nose pets as Rebecca ignites Sleeptime Pillow Pet's stars across the ceiling. Lying in bed together, they count the stars, make wishes. The wishes are secret, of course, but Rebecca's is that they will transform the nursery into a playroom for Maddy.

It is time, finally, for nighttime affirmations, Rebecca whispering each well-loved phrase with her daughter while Mark watches them with silent adoration.

"My voice matters," Maddy and Rebecca say.

"I tried my best today," they say.

"I am still growing and learning."

"I have what it takes."

I have what it takes, Rebecca repeats again in her head, and then she is welling up, welling up with happiness, so much it spills out of her, and Mark hugs her from one side and Maddy from the other, and it is everything she will ever need, just them, the three of them, a holy little trinity.

About the Author

Photo © Melissa Hurwitz

Gregg Hurwitz is the #1 international bestselling author of the *Orphan X* series and sixteen other thrillers. His critically acclaimed novels have appeared on multiple top-ten lists and have been published in thirty-three languages. Hurwitz has sold scripts to many of the major Hollywood film studios and has written, developed, and produced television for various networks. He lives in Los Angeles.